AGATHA RAISIN and the WITCH of WYCKHADDEN

An Agatha Raisin Cotswolds murder-mystery

M. C. Beaton

ROBINSON
London

Constable & Robinson Ltd
3 The Lanchesters
162 Fulham Palace Road
London W6 9ER
www.constablerobinson.com

First published in the USA 1999 by St Martin's Press
175 Fifth Avenue, New York, NY 10010

First UK edition published by Robinson,
an imprint of Constable & Robinson Ltd 2006

This paperback edition published by Robinson,
an imprint of Constable & Robinson Ltd 2009

A copy of the British Library Cataloguing in Publication data is available from the British Library

ISBN: 978-1-84529-356-7

Printed and bound in the EU

7 9 10 8 6

AGATHA RAISIN
and the
WITCH of WYCKHADDEN

The Agatha Raisin series
(listed in order)

Agatha Raisin and the Quiche of Death
Agatha Raisin and the Vicious Vet
Agatha Raisin and the Potted Gardener
Agatha Raisin and the Walkers of Dembley
Agatha Raisin and the Murderous Marriage
Agatha Raisin and the Terrible Tourist
Agatha Raisin and the Wellspring of Death
Agatha Raisin and the Wizard of Evesham
Agatha Raisin and the Witch of Wyckhadden
Agatha Raisin and the Fairies of Fryfam
Agatha Raisin and the Love from Hell
Agatha Raisin and the Day the Floods Came
Agatha Raisin and the Curious Curate
Agatha Raisin and the Haunted House
Agatha Raisin and the Deadly Dance
Agatha Raisin and the Perfect Paragon
Agatha Raisin and Love, Lies and Liquor
Agatha Raisin and Kissing Christmas Goodbye
Agatha Raisin and a Spoonful of Poison
Agatha Raisin: There Goes the Bride

For Gladwen Williams of Norton Lindsey
with affection

AGATHA RAISIN

Agatha Raisin was born in a tower block slum in Birmingham and christened Agatha Styles. No middle names. Agatha had often longed for at least two middle names such as Caroline or Olivia. Her parents, Joseph and Margaret Styles, were both unemployed and both drunks. They lived on benefits and the occasional bout of shoplifting.

Agatha attended the local comprehensive as a rather shy and sensitive child but quickly developed a bullying, aggressive manner so that the other pupils would steer clear of her.

At the age of fifteen, her parents decided it was time she earned her keep and her mother found her work in a biscuit factory, checking packets of biscuits on a conveyer belt for any faults.

As soon as Agatha had squirreled away enough money, she ran off to London and found work as a waitress and studied computing at evening classes. But she fell in love with a customer at the restaurant, Jimmy Raisin. Jimmy had curly black hair and bright blue eyes and a great deal of charm. He seemed to have plenty of money to throw around. He wanted an affair, but besotted as she was, Agatha held out for marriage.

They moved into one room in a lodging house in Finsbury Park where Jimmy's money soon ran out (he would never say where it came from in the first place). And he drank. Agatha found she had escaped the frying pan into the fire.

She was fiercely ambitious. One night, when she came home and found Jimmy stretched out on the bed dead drunk, she packed her things and escaped.

She found work as a secretary at a public relations firm and soon moved into doing public relations herself. Her mixture of bullying and cajoling brought her success. She saved and saved until she could start her own business.

But Agatha had always been a dreamer. Years back when she had been a child her parents had taken her on one glorious holiday. They had rented a cottage in the Cotswolds for a week. Agatha never forgot that golden holiday or the beauty of the countryside.

So as soon as she had amassed a great deal of money, she took early retirement and bought a cottage in the village of Carsely in the Cotswolds.

Her first attempt at detective work came after she cheated at a village quiche baking competition by putting a shop bought quiche in as her own. The judge died of poisoning and shamed Agatha had to find the real killer. Her adventures there are covered in the first Agatha Raisin mystery, *The Quiche of Death*, and in the series of novels that follow. As successful as she is in detecting, she constantly remains unlucky in love. Will she ever find happiness with the man of her dreams? Watch this space!

Chapter One

There is nothing more depressing for a middle-aged lovelorn woman with bald patches on her head than to find herself in an English seaside resort out of season. Wind ripped along the promenade, sending torn posters advertising summer jollities flapping, and huge waves sent spray high into the air.

Agatha had lost her hair when a vengeful hairdresser had applied depilatory to it rather than shampoo. It had grown back in tufts but leaving distressingly bare patches of scalp. Not wishing the love of her life, James Lacey, to return from his travels and find her in such a mess, Agatha had fled from Carsely to this seaside resort of Wyckhadden to wait for her hair to grow.

She had booked into the Garden Hotel, advertised as small but exclusive. She now wished she had chosen somewhere plastic and bright and modern. The Garden Hotel had not changed much since Victorian times. The ceilings were high, the carpets thick, and the walls very solid, so that it was as hushed and quiet as a tomb. The other residents were elderly, and no one feels more uncomfortable among the elderly than a middle-aged woman who is rapidly approaching that stage of life herself. Agatha could suddenly understand why middle-aged men often blossomed out in jeans, high boots and leather jackets and went looking for a young thing to wear on their arm. She walked a lot, determined to lose weight and remain supple.

One look around the dining-room of the Garden at her fellow guests made her start to ponder the sense of getting a face-lift.

The town of Wyckhadden had prospered during a boom in the late nineteenth century, and its popularity had continued well into the twentieth, but with the advent of cheap foreign travel, holiday-makers had declined. Why holiday in Britain in the rain when sunny Spain was only an hour's plane flight away?

So on this windy day, two days after her arrival, she was charging along a deserted promenade, head down against the wind, wondering how soon she could find a sheltered spot to enjoy a cigarette and get some of the excess of oxygen out of her lungs.

She turned away from the restless sound of the heaving sea and made her way up a narrow cobbled street where the original fishermen's cottages had now all been painted pastel colours like in an Italian village and had cute names like Home At Last, Dunroamin, The Refuge and so on, showing that they had been bought by retired wealthy people. Tourism might be on the wane, but property prices in seaside resorts in the south of England were high.

She came to a tea-shop and was about to go in when she saw the non-smoking sign on the door. The government was planning to ban smoking in pubs, Agatha had read in the newspapers. Not a word about the dangers of alcohol, she thought, as a particularly strong gust of wind sent her reeling. People who smoked did not drive off the road or go home and beat up their wives. Drunks did. And with the fumes from more and more cars polluting the air, she thought that smoking had become a political issue. The left were anti-smoking, the right pro-smoking, and the lot in the middle who had given up smoking wanted everyone to suffer.

She saw a pub on the corner called the Dog and Duck. It looked old and pretty, white-washed with black beams and hanging baskets which swung in the wind. She pushed open the door and went in.

Inside belied the outside. It was dark and gloomy: stained tables, linoleum on the floor, and if there was any heating at all she could not feel it.

She had wanted a coffee, and pubs these days sold coffee, but she felt so low she ordered a double gin and tonic instead. 'We don't have ice,' said the bartender.

'You don't need it,' snapped Agatha. 'This place is freezing.'

'You're the only one that's complained,' he said, scooping up her money.

Should be written on the British flag, thought Agatha sourly. 'You're the only one that's complained' was always the answer to the slightly less than timid customer who dared to complain about anything.

Perhaps she should admit defeat and go home. She lit a cigarette. The pub was nearly empty. There was only she herself and a couple talking in low voices in a corner, holding hands and looking at each other with the sad intensity of adulterers. They probably met here, thought Agatha, knowing that no one they knew would see them.

There must be some sort of life in this town.

The pub door swung open and a tall man came in. Agatha studied him as he went up to the bar. He was wearing a long dark overcoat. He had a lugubrious face and large pale eyes under heavy lids. His hair was black, like patent leather, smooth across his head. He ordered a drink and then turned and looked curiously at Agatha. He was far from an Adonis, and yet Agatha was suddenly conscious of her face, reddened by the wind, and her head tied up in a headscarf because she had not wanted to wear her wig.

He walked up to her table and loomed over her. 'Are you visiting?' he asked.

'Yes,' said Agatha curtly.

'You've picked a bad time of year for it.'

'I've picked a bad place,' retorted Agatha. 'I think people only come here to die.'

His pale eyes gleamed with amusement. 'Oh, we have our fun. There's dancing in the pier ballroom tonight.' He sat down opposite her.

'How on earth do people get to it?' asked Agatha. 'Surely anyone trying to get along the pier in this weather would be blown away.'

'I tell you what. I'll take you.'

'I don't know you!'

He held out a hand. 'Jimmy Jessop.'

'Well, Mr Jessop . . .'

'Jimmy.'

'Jimmy, then. I'm a bit old to be picked up in a crummy pub by someone I don't know.'

He seemed amused by her glaring eyes and haughty manner. 'If you normally go on like this you can't have any fun at all. If you go to a dance with me, what terrible thing could happen to you? I am probably the same age as you, so I'm hardly going to try to take off my clothes and rape you.'

'You don't need to take off all your clothes to rape someone.'

'I wouldn't know, never having tried it.'

Agatha suddenly thought of another gloomy evening alone at the Garden.

'Oh, why not. I'm Agatha Raisin. Mrs Agatha Raisin. I'm staying at the Garden Hotel.'

'And is there a Mr Raisin?'

'Dead.'

'I'm sorry.'

'I'm not.'

He looked surprised but then he said, 'I'll pick you up at eight o'clock. The pier's close to your hotel, so we can walk. Want another one?' He pointed to her empty glass.

'No, I'd best get back.' Agatha just wanted to escape from him, to return to the hotel and figure out whether she should really go. If she changed her mind, she could always ask reception to tell him that she was indisposed.

She gathered up her handbag and gloves. He stood up and held the door open for her.

'Till tonight,' he said. Agatha mumbled something and scurried out past him.

Back in her hotel room, she stood before the long glass on the wardrobe door and studied her reflection to see if there was anything about her that should make some strange man invite her out. Her head was tightly wrapped in a headscarf, her face without make-up was shiny and her nose was still pink with the cold. Her eyes looked even smaller than usual. She took off her coat and unwound her headscarf and looked dismally at the tufts of hair on her head. No, he must be weird. She would not go.

She looked at her watch. It was nearly lunch-time. She washed her face and then sat down at the dressing-table – kidney-shaped, with a triple mirror and a green silk flounce to match the slippery green silk cover on the large bed. A flapper's dressing-table, thought Agatha. She wondered whether there was any new furniture in the hotel at all. She carefully applied make-up and then put on a glossy brown wig. Not bad, she thought. Now if Jimmy Jessop had seen her looking like this . . .

She gathered up her handbag again and then a paperback as a barrier in case any of the geriatrics in the dining-room tried to start up a conversation, and made her way down the thickly carpeted stairs with their brass risers. A fitful gleam of sunshine stabbed down through a large stained-glass window on the landing, chequering the Turkey-red carpet on the stairs with harlequin colours.

The dining-room was high-ceilinged with long windows overlooking the sea.

She took a table in the corner and covertly surveyed the other diners. There was an elderly man whom the waitresses addressed as Colonel. He had a good head of snowy-white hair and a lined, tanned face. He was tall and upright and wearing an old but well-cut tweed jacket. Glancing over at him and obviously trying to catch his attention was a lady with improbably blonde hair. She was heavily powdered and her lipstick was a screaming red. She was wearing a low-cut blouse which showed too much shrivelled and freckled neck. There was another man, small and crabby-looking with a dowager's hump. Then two elderly women, one tall and masculine in tweeds, the other small, weedy and rabbity-looking.

What an advertisement for euthanasia, thought Agatha sourly.

The food when it arrived was good, solid English cooking. That day the main course was pork tenderloin glazed with honey, served with apple sauce, onions, roast potatoes, boiled potatoes, cauliflower cheese and peas.

It was followed by toffee pudding and lashings of Devon cream. Agatha ate the lot, and she groaned as she could feel the band of her skirt tightening. She would need to go for another long walk or she would feel lethargic and heavy for the rest of the day.

This time, as the tide had gone out, she went down on to the shingly beach where great grey-green waves crashed and surged.

She had a sudden memory of a piece of poetry learned at school.

> But now I only hear
> Its melancholy, long, withdrawing roar,
> Retreating, to the breath
> Of the night-wind, down the vast edges
> drear
> And naked shingles of the world

Agatha brightened. It was grand to be able to remember things, if only a fragment of poetry. That was one of her fears, that her memories would be lost to her one day.

There was something hypnotic about the rise and fall of the waves. The wind was slowly dropping and pale sunlight gilded the restless sea. She walked miles before she turned back to the hotel, feeling energetic and refreshed. She may as well go to the dance on the pier with the mysterious Jimmy Jessop. It was unexpected, a little adventure.

Her mind was thoroughly made up when the blonde woman met her in the reception area and fluted, 'We haven't been introduced. I am Mrs Daisy Jones.'

Agatha held out her hand. 'Agatha Raisin.'

'Well, Miss Raisin . . .'

'Mrs.'

'Mrs Raisin. The colonel, that is dear Colonel Lyche, has suggested we all get together after dinner for a game of Scrabble. There are so few of us. Miss Jennifer Stobbs and Miss Mary Dulsey are very keen players. And Mr Harry Berry usually beats us all.'

'Too kind,' said Agatha, backing away, 'but I've got a date.'

'I thought you were a business woman when I saw you. I said to the colonel –'

'I mean a date. A fellow.'

'Oh, really. Another time, then.'

Agatha escaped up to her room. Surely a dance on the pier was infinitely preferable to an evening playing Scrabble with that lot!

At seven o'clock, she picked up the phone and ordered sandwiches and a bottle of mineral water to be served to her in her room.

When the elderly waiter creaked in with it ten minutes later, Agatha tipped him lavishly because he looked too old and frail to be carrying one of the heavy solid-silver trays the hotel used for room service.

She ate quickly and then put on an evening blouse and a black velvet skirt. She carefully put on her wig and made up her face. Then she swung open the wardrobe door. The wardrobe could have been turned into a room in another type of hotel, she thought. It was one of those vast Victorian mahogany ones. Hanging there was her mink coat. She took it out, her hands caressing the fur. Should she wear it? Or would some animal libber spit at her and try to wrench it off her back? Or was it safe to consign it to the perils of the pier ballroom cloakroom? If she put on a cloth coat, then she would need to wear a cardigan over her evening blouse. With a feeling of sin, she wrapped it round her, remembering when she had bought it in the dear, dead days when fur was fashionable. Then she tied a silk scarf over her wig to anchor it. The wind might rise again.

When she went downstairs, Jimmy was

waiting in the reception, wearing white evening shirt and black tie under another long black coat.

'Dressy affair?' asked Agatha.

'We always dress up in Wyckhadden,' he said. 'We're pretty old-fashioned.'

'What kind of dancing is it?' asked Agatha. 'Disco?'

'No, ballroom.'

As they walked along the pier, Agatha saw a poster. BALLROOM DANCING FOR THE OLD-TYMERS, it said. And then in smaller letters, 'Old-Age Pensioners, Half-Price.'

This place'll make me old before my time, thought Agatha, and suddenly wished she had not come.

They checked their coats in at the desk and then walked into the ballroom. The dancers were all middle-aged or elderly, performing a lively military Two-Step. 'Shall we?' asked Jimmy.

Agatha looked longingly at the bar. 'I could do with a drink first.'

'Right you are.' He led her over to the bar. 'Gin and tonic?'

Agatha nodded. He collected their drinks and they sat down at a small table next to the dance floor.

A couple came up to join them, a tall red-head with big hair, big bosoms and hard eyes so mascaraed that they looked as if two spiders were resting on her face. Her partner was small, wearing a bright red jacket and white trousers. ''Ow's our Jimmy?' asked the redhead.

'Agatha,' said Jimmy, 'this is Maisie and Chris Leeman. Agatha Raisin.'

'Mind if we join you?' asked Maisie, and she and Chris drew up chairs and sat down as well without being asked. 'Fetch me a brandy and Babycham, Chris, there's a love,' said Maisie. She turned to Agatha. 'I haven't seen you before.'

'I'm on holiday,' said Agatha.

'Where you staying?'

'The Garden.'

'Oh, there's posh for you.' She nudged Jimmy in the ribs. 'Got yourself a rich widow, eh?'

What awful people, thought Agatha. If only I could escape. Chris came back with drinks. He asked Agatha what she was doing in Wyckhadden and Agatha explained again that she was on holiday.

'Odd place for a holiday. Most people come here to die.' Chris nudged Maisie in the ribs and she shrieked with laughter.

'Dance, Agatha?' asked Jimmy.

'Yes, please.' Agatha rose from the table and gratefully joined Jimmy in the Saint Bernard's waltz. Why am I such a snob? she fretted. But I really can't bear Chris and Maisie and if that's the kind of friends he has, I don't want to see any more of him after this evening.

Jimmy was dancing expertly and exchanging greetings with other couples on the floor. He seemed to know an awful lot of people, but then Wyckhadden was a small place. 'Have you lived here very long?' asked Agatha, executing a neat pirouette. Amazing how the steps came back to one.

'All my life,' he said.

'I never asked you if you were married.'

'I was,' said Jimmy. 'She died.'

'Long ago?'

'Ten years.'

'Any children?'

'Two. I've a son of twenty-eight and a daughter of thirty-two.'

'And what do they do?' asked Agatha, wondering if she could steer him away from Chris and Maisie after this dance finished.

'John, my son, is an engineer. Not married. Joan is married to a university lecturer at Essex University. Got two kids. Very happy.'

The dance finished. A tango was announced. To her relief, Agatha could see Chris and Maisie taking the floor.

They sat down again. A couple danced past. 'Taking a night off from the villains, Jimmy?' called the woman.

He laughed and nodded.

'What did she mean?' asked Agatha.

'I'm a police inspector.'

Agatha's eyes gleamed. 'I'm by way of being an amateur detective,' she said. She proceeded to give him several highly embroidered accounts of her various 'cases'. She was so carried away by her stories that she failed to notice he was looking more and more uncomfortable.

She was just in the middle of what she considered a highly enthralling account of a murder case she had been involved in when Chris and Maisie returned to the table.

'Care to dance, Maisie?' asked Jimmy, seemingly unaware that Agatha was in mid-sentence.

Agatha turned a mortified pink as Jimmy led Maisie on to the floor. 'Dance?' suggested Chris.

'Why not?' replied Agatha gloomily.

Chris turned out to be one of those showy ballroom dancers, all swoops and glides that seemed to have nothing to do with the music. He smelt so strongly of Old Spice that Agatha figured he must have bathed in the stuff.

For the rest of the evening, Jimmy kept introducing Agatha to couples and somehow Agatha ended up dancing with the man while Jimmy danced off with the woman. Agatha was hurt. A police inspector should have been delighted to find out she was a fellow crime buster.

At last the evening was over. Jimmy helped Agatha into her mink coat and led her outside. The wind had risen again. Ferocious gusts swept the pier and the lights that decorated it bobbed and ducked in the wind. Agatha scrabbled in her coat pocket for her silk scarf. But as she took it out and tried to put it on her head, the wind snatched it from her hands and sent it dancing into the sea.

'Oh, dear,' mourned Agatha. 'That was my best scarf.'

'What?' he shouted, trying to make himself heard above the scream of the wind and the thundering of the sea.

'I said . . .' And then Agatha let out another scream. For a really treacherous gust of wind snatched off her wig. It caught on the rail of the pier and she ran to rescue it. But just as she was reaching for it, another gust of wind loosened it from the rail and it was carried away into the roaring blackness of the night.

She walked back to Jimmy, drawing her collar up as far around her ears as she could. The swinging lights of the pier illuminated the wreck of her own hair.

'I've lost my wig,' mourned Agatha.

'My wife died of cancer,' shouted Jimmy.

'It's not cancer,' wailed Agatha.

They scurried in silence, side by side, to Agatha's hotel. Agatha said in the shelter of the porticoed entrance, 'Thank you for a pleasant evening. Forgive me for not asking you in for a drink, but I am very tired.'

'I hope you enjoy the rest of your holiday,' he said stiffly, and with that he turned and left. Mrs Daisy Jones was in the reception as Agatha, head down, scuttled for the stairs.

'Good evening, Mrs Raisin.'

Agatha grunted by way of reply and scurried up the stairs. She dived into her room like an animal into its burrow. Sanctuary. What a horrible evening. And that wig had cost a fortune.

She had a feeling of panic. What on earth was she doing trapped in this hotel? She would check out tomorrow and move on.

In the morning, Agatha was just finishing her breakfast when she saw Daisy Jones heading for her table. Agatha raised a copy of the *Daily Mail* as a barrier, but undeterred, Daisy said cheerfully, 'I couldn't help noticing your hair last night. What happened?'

'It's the result of a nervous illness,' said Agatha, who no longer wanted to brag about her exploits.

Daisy sat down and leaned over the table. Thick white powder filled the seams and cracks in her face and her small thin mouth was heavily painted. 'I know someone who can help you,' she whispered.

'I'm told by doctors that my hair will soon grow back,' said Agatha defiantly. Her head was now wrapped up in a blue scarf.

'Have you heard of Francie Juddle?'

'Who's she?' asked Agatha.

'Well . . .' Daisy gave a little titter and looked furtively around. 'She's the local witch, but she performs wonders. She took away Mary Dulsey's warts.'

'And where does this witch live?'

'The pink cottage in Partons Lane, just at the far end of the town. If you walk to the very end of the promenade and turn left, you'll find it. It's the third cottage up from the sea.'

'Thank you,' said Agatha politely but dismissively.

'Do try her. She has occult powers. We are having another game of Scrabble tonight in the lounge after dinner. Please join us.'

'If I'm free,' said Agatha, picking up the paper again.

When Daisy had left, Agatha found her curiosity about this witch was roused. A visit to her would liven up the day. Besides, the very thought of packing and moving on somewhere else filled her with lethargy.

Half an hour later, wrapped up in her mink coat, she made her way along the promenade. It was a steel-grey day without a breath of wind. Great glassy waves curled on the shingle and then retreated with a long dragging sound.

The evening before flashed before her mind. At least she could not think that Jimmy had gone off her when she lost her wig. He had gone off her long before that. Her old determination and energy were returning. By the time she returned to Carsely, James Lacey would see a happy, healthy Agatha with a full head of hair. In various Victorian iron-and-glass shelters along the promenade, the elderly huddled together, staring out at the sea. They're waiting for Death to arrive, thought Agatha with a shudder. Come in, Number Nine, your time's up.

She hurried past them, her head down. At the end of the promenade was Partons Lane. She walked up to a pink cottage and knocked at the door with the knocker which was a brass devil's head.

After a few moments the door was opened by a plump little woman with smooth features and light-grey eyes. She had thick black hair worn up in a French pleat.

'Yes?'

For one brief second, Agatha forgot Daisy's name. Then her face cleared. 'Daisy Jones at the Garden Hotel suggested you might be able to help me.'

'You're supposed to phone for an appointment,' said Francie Juddle. 'But you're in luck. Mrs Braithwaite was supposed to call, but she died.'

Agatha blinked in surprise but followed her in.

She expected to be led into some sort of dark sanctum dominated by a black-velvet-draped table with a crystal ball on top, but she found herself in a cosy little parlour with some good pieces of furniture, a bright fire, and a large cat, white, not black, sleeping on a hooked rug in front of it.

'Sit down,' said Francie, nodding in the direction of a winged armchair beside the fire. Agatha sat down, first removing her mink coat. 'You shouldn't be wearing a thing like that,' said Francie.

'Why?'

'Think of all the little animals that died to keep you warm.'

'I didn't come here for a lecture on animals' liberation.'

Francie settled herself in a chair opposite Agatha. She had very short legs in pale glassy stockings.

'So how can I help you?'

Agatha unwound the scarf from her head. 'Look at this.'

'What happened?'

'Some wretched woman shampooed me with depilatory. It should be growing back.'

'Oh, I've got something that'll fix that,' Francie said, smiling.

'Could I have some?' asked Agatha impatiently.

'Of course. Eighty pounds.'

'What!'

'It'll cost eighty pounds.'

'That's a lot,' said Agatha, 'for something that might not work.'

'It'll work.'

'I suppose people come to you about all sorts of things,' said Agatha.

'Everything from warts to love potions.'

'Love potions! Surely there isn't such a thing.'

'There is.'

'Francie, it is Francie, isn't it? . . . We're both business women. I've spent a fortune on cosmetics which claim to reduce wrinkles and they don't, lipsticks which are supposed to be kiss-proof and aren't, so why should I believe in your hair restorer?'

Francie's eyes twinkled. 'You'll never know until you try.'

'How much is the love potion?'

'Twenty pounds.'

'So love comes cheaper than hair restorer.'

'You could say that.'

'But,' said Agatha, 'if this hair restorer works, you could be making a fortune.'

'I could be making a fortune out of a lot of my potions if I decided to go into the manufacturing business, but then I would have all the headache of factories and staff.'

'Not necessarily,' said the ever-shrewd Agatha. 'All you need to do is sell the recipe for millions.'

'I am expecting a client soon. Do you want the stuff or not?'

Agatha hesitated. But the thought that her hair might never grow back again was beginning to make her feel panicky. 'All right,' she said gruffly, 'and I'll take the love potion as well.'

Francie rose and went out of the room. Agatha rose as well and went to the small window and looked out. Sunlight was beginning to gild the cobbles outside. The wind had risen again. She was beginning to feel silly. What if she gave James Lacey the love potion and it made him sick?

Francie came back with two bottles, one small and one large. 'The small one is the love potion and the large one is for your hair,' she said. 'Apply the hair restorer every night before you go to bed. Put five drops of the love potion in his drink. Are you a widow?'

'Yes.'

'I give seances. I can get you in touch with the dear departed.'

'He's departed but not dear.'

'That'll be one hundred pounds.'

'I don't have that amount of cash on me.'

'A cheque will do.'

Agatha took out her cheque-book and rested it on a small table. 'Do I make it out to Frances Juddle?'

'Please.'

Agatha wrote out the cheque and handed it to her. Then she put on her coat, picked up the two bottles and put them in her handbag and made for the door.

'Get rid of that coat,' said Francie. 'It's a disgrace.'

Agatha glared at her, and left without replying. How could anyone know what that coat meant to her? It had been her first expensive purchase ever, after she had clawed her way out of the Birmingham slum in which she had been born and climbed the ladder of success. To her, the coat had been like gleaming armour, signalling the arrival of a new rich Agatha Raisin. And that had been in the days before wearing fur was considered a sin.

Outside, the sun was shining down and people were walking about, quite a number of them young. It was as if Wyckhadden had suddenly come to life. Agatha decided to go back to that pub where she had met Jimmy. She could not bear the fact that he had suddenly and inexplicably gone off her.

She pushed open the door of the pub. It was the lunch-hour and it was busy with office workers. But she found an empty table and sat down after collecting a gin and tonic from the bar.

Unless she hurried, she would miss lunch at the hotel and she did not feel like trying any of the pub food, which smelled horrible. She finished her gin and tonic just as the pub door opened and Jimmy came in. He shot her a brief look and then turned around and walked out.

Agatha felt quite weepy. But then, she consoled herself, she had thought him weird the way he had picked her up. So why should she be surprised by his odd behaviour?

She walked back out into the sunshine, but glad of the warmth of her coat, for the wind was cold.

She was making her way towards the hotel when she passed a group of young people who were sitting on a wall drinking beer and eating hamburgers. One of them, a young girl with noserings and earrings, suddenly flew at Agatha, clawing at her coat and screaming, 'Murderer.'

Alarmed, Agatha gave her an almighty push and sent her flying and then set off at a run.

Once in the hotel, she hurried up to her room and lovingly hung the precious coat away in the wardrobe.

Enough was enough. One more day and she would check out.

After dinner, she reluctantly joined the other guests in the lounge, where the colonel was opening the Scrabble board.

The tall masculine woman turned out to be Miss Jennifer Stobbs and the small weedy one, Miss Mary Dulsey. The old crabby man, Harry Berry, smelt of mothballs and peppermints. Daisy Jones was flirting coyly with Colonel Lyche.

'So few guests,' said Agatha.

'We're all residents, apart from you,' said Jennifer. She had a heavy, sallow face with a bristle of hairs above her upper lip. Her hair, streaked with grey, was close-cropped. 'Get a lot of guests in the season and at weekends.'

'Are you any good at Scrabble, Agatha?' asked the colonel. Agatha was momentarily startled by the use of her first name. The members of the old-fashioned ladies' society in her home village of Carsely addressed one another as Mrs this and Miss that.

'Average,' said Agatha, and then remembered dismally the cosy evenings spent with James playing Scrabble when they had been engaged.

She played as well as she could, but the others were not only dedicated Scrabble players but also crossword addicts, and so Agatha did badly compared to them.

'Did you go to Francie?' asked Daisy.

But Agatha was already ashamed of having spent one hundred pounds on what she believed was probably two bottles of coloured water and so she lied and said, 'No.'

'Oh, you should, she's very good.'

Another game started. Agatha tried harder this time but still had the lowest score. 'That's it for this evening,' said Colonel Lyche. Agatha was surprised to find out it was just after midnight.

She refused the colonel's offer of a drink and went up to her room, thinking that they had all been good company, and once you got to know the elderly, it was amazing how much younger they became.

She took off her blouse and put it in her laundry bag. Then she removed her skirt and went to the massive wardrobe to hang it up.

She swung open the door.

Then she screamed.

Chapter Two

Her beloved mink coat was hanging in shreds and it had been daubed with red paint.

She backed away from the wreck of it. Agatha found she was trembling. She clenched her shaking hands and then was overtaken with an outburst of anger. There would only be the night porter on duty. She would call the police. She looked up the local phone book, pressed '9' for an outside line and dialled Wyckhadden police station.

'Evening, Wyckhadden police,' said a bored voice.

Agatha curtly snapped out the details of the desecration of her fur coat. 'Anything else damaged?' asked the voice, still as bored.

Agatha looked wildly around the room. 'Not that I can see.'

'Don't touch anything. We'll have someone along directly.'

Agatha began to look around the room. Nothing else seemed to have been touched.

Even her jewel case, open on the dressing-table, still had all her pieces of jewellery in it.

She called the night porter and explained tersely what had happened and that she had called the police. 'I'll be up right away,' he said.

After a few moments, there was a knock at her door. The night porter was young for an establishment such as the Garden Hotel, being somewhere in his forties. He had an unhealthy open-pored grey face, a droopy moustache and dyed black hair. He stared in awe at the wreckage of Agatha's coat. 'Did you forget to lock your room?' he asked.

'I did not forget. I was playing Scrabble with the others. I locked my door and kept the key in my handbag.'

'Some of our residents are very forgetful,' he said.

'I am not senile!' howled Agatha. 'If I say I locked my door, then that is what I did!'

Elderly people do not sleep very well and somehow the other residents must have sensed something was going on. The door to Agatha's room was open. Mrs Daisy Jones, wrapped in a pink silk quilted dressing-gown, appeared, peering in, shortly followed by the colonel, still dressed. They both exclaimed in horror over the vandalism.

'I blame the welfare system,' said the colonel. 'They've got young people down here who've never done a day's work in their lives.' The rest of the residents soon crowded in, chattering and exclaiming.

'I think you should all go away,' said Agatha desperately. 'The police will want to dust the room for fingerprints.'

'Which of you is Mrs Raisin?' called a voice from the doorway. The residents parted to reveal a squat burly man in a tight suit and anorak and a policewoman who looked as if she was half asleep.

The residents shuffled out into the corridor. 'Detective Constable Ian Tarret,' said the man, shutting the door on the elderly residents. 'This the coat?'

'That *was* the coat,' said Agatha bitterly.

'Let's begin at the beginning, Mrs Raisin. You are a visitor?'

'Yes. I've only been here a few days.'

'Why Wyckhadden? Know people here?'

'No, I wanted somewhere for a holiday, that was all.'

'Have you worn the coat since your arrival?'

'Yes, I wore it to a dance on the pier last night. I went with Inspector Jimmy Jessop.'

'I thought you didn't know anyone in Wyckhadden.'

'He picked me up in a pub,' said Agatha, and despite her distress she maliciously hoped that bit of gossip would get round the police station.

'Now, there are people around who attack women wearing fur. Anyone have a go at you?'

'Yes, this morning, on the prom, just before I got to the hotel. There were some young people sitting on a wall. A girl with spiky hair, noserings and earrings attacked me.'

'Didn't you report it?'

'Would you have done anything about it?'

'Certainly. You should have reported it. Anyone else make adverse comments?'

Agatha thought guiltily of the witch of Wyckhadden, Francie Juddle. She did not like to confess she had been consulting a witch. And what if it came out that she had asked for a love potion?

'No,' she lied.

'We'll have the fingerprint men along in the morning.'

'Why the morning? Why not now?'

'We're a bit pushed. Lots of work.'

'A crime wave in Wyckhadden?'

'It's not that. It's lack of funds. We're only a small station. The forensic boys have to come from Hadderton, the main town. Perhaps you'd like to drop into the station in the morning and make a full statement.'

'Yes,' said Agatha wearily.

'Is the coat insured?'

'No. I mean if I'd been at home it might have come under the house-contents insurance, but I never thought of taking out travel insurance to go to a place like this.'

'You'll know better next time,' he said in a heavy, sententious way that made Agatha want to hit him.

Agatha looked at the policewoman. She was sitting on the bed, her chin drooped on her chest, her eyes closed. 'Your policewoman's asleep,' she said.

'Constable Trul!' barked Tarret.

'I wasn't asleep,' she said. 'I was thinking.'

Tarret turned to the night porter. 'We'll go downstairs. You'd better tell us who could have had access to a key to this room.'

Agatha saw them out. She felt like a drink but this hotel was too old-fashioned to have anything modern like a minibar. She slumped down in a chair. She shouldn't have lied about her visit to Francie. Her eyes narrowed. It was Francie who had criticized her coat. Such as that horrible girl on the prom who had attacked her would hardly stroll into an expensive hotel. Her mind made feverish by the wreck of her coat, Agatha suddenly decided it could not have been anyone else but Francie. The residents of the hotel had all been playing Scrabble with her. Daisy Jones had left at one point to 'powder her nose', as she delicately put it, but she had gone in the direction of the Ladies on the ground floor. Then the colonel and Mr Berry had left the game on two occasions to buy drinks. But by no stretch of the imagination could she imagine either elderly gentleman nipping up the stairs to slash her coat.

It must be that dreadful Francie, Francie who was probably lying in smug sleep at that very moment.

Agatha decided to go and wake her up. If she was the culprit, then she might still have some evidence of red paint on her hands or under her fingernails.

She put on a warm anorak and headed downstairs. Tarret and Trul were still questioning the night porter. 'Got to get a breath of air,' gabbled Agatha.

As she walked along the deserted promenade under a small chilly moon, she felt that if she could solve The Case Of The Vandalized Mink Coat, that would show Jimmy Jessop she was a brain to be reckoned with.

The night was very still and the silence of the town, eerie. Her own footsteps sounded unnaturally loud.

Her courage was beginning to fail. What if Francie didn't answer the door? What if the neighbours reported her to the police? But the thought of impressing the hitherto unimpressed Jimmy spurred her on.

As she turned into Partons Lane, she noticed that the street light at the corner was out, making the entrance to the lane pitch-black. She stumbled slightly on the cobbles. Getting to the pink cottage, she raised her hand and knocked loudly on the door. The door gave and swung slowly open.

Agatha felt superstitious dread flooding her. It was as if the witch had known she was coming and had magically caused the door to open. She went inside. 'Francie!' she called.

The witch was no doubt upstairs asleep. Agatha fumbled around the hall looking for a light switch and at last found one at the foot of the stairs. Feeling more confident and thinking it might be an idea to surprise Francie asleep and study her fingernails and hands before waking her, Agatha started to creep up the stairs, which were as thickly carpeted as those at the hotel.

She gingerly pushed open one door. The bathroom. She tried another. A box-room. Another door. In the light from the stairs, Agatha could see it was a bedroom. She felt around inside the door for a light switch, found it, and clicked it on.

Lying half in, half out of the bed was Francie Juddle. Blood from a great wound on her head had dripped on to the white carpet, leaving a dark stain. The white cat was crouched on the edge of the bed. When it saw Agatha, with one spring it flew straight at her face. Agatha screamed and tore it off.

Her first instinct was to flee. But Francie might still be alive. Agatha could not bring herself to touch the body. There was a phone extension by the bed. Fingerprints, she thought. My fingerprints will be everywhere. Why didn't I wear gloves? How do I explain my call?

She had forgotten the number of the police station. She dialled 999 and in a trembling voice asked for police and ambulance and then went down to the small hall to wait.

Agatha wished from the bottom of her heart that she had never left Carsely. She crouched in a small chair in the hall. It would come out that she had visited Francie. And how was she to explain what she was doing at Francie's cottage at this time of night?

She heard car doors slam outside the cottage. Detective Constable Tarret came in followed by his sleepy policewoman.

'What is this about?' he demanded. 'What are you doing here?'

'It's Mrs Juddle,' said Agatha. 'She's upstairs in the bedroom. I think she's dead.'

The ambulance men came in at that moment.

'Show us,' said Tarret.

Agatha led the way upstairs and to the bedroom, pointed at the door and stood back while the police and the ambulance men went in. Jimmy Jessop came up the stairs.

He glanced at her. 'In there,' said Agatha faintly.

She retreated to the hall. Soon the scene-of-crime men arrived with their equipment, then the pathologist with his black bag. Francie must be dead, thought Agatha. There was no rush to bring her out to the ambulance. More police arrived to cordon off the outside of the cottage.

Agatha began to wonder whether she should slip off back to the hotel. After all, they would know where to find her. But she stayed where she was. The trembling had stopped and now she felt exhausted.

Inspector Jimmy Jessop came down the stairs. 'I'd better ask you to accompany us back to the station,' he said. 'Constable Trul will take you there.' His eyes were flat and expressionless.

The policewoman came down the stairs. Lights were on in all the neighbouring cottages. As she was led out, a flashlight went off in Agatha's face. The local press had arrived. Agatha cringed and tried to hide her face. She got in the car. Another flashlight went off.

Numb now with shock and exhaustion, Agatha was borne off to the police station and put in an interviewing room. Constable Trul brought her a cup of milky tea and a digestive biscuit and then sat in the corner, her hands folded in her lap.

Agatha sipped the tea and wrinkled her nose in disgust. It was the sort of stuff in a thin paper cup that came out of a machine. She pushed it away and laid her head on the desk and immediately fell asleep. She was awakened three quarters of an hour later by someone shaking her shoulder. It was Jimmy Jessop. She looked up at him blearily.

'Now, Mrs Raisin,' he said, 'let's get this over with. We all need our sleep.'

Agatha sat up, blinked and looked around. Jimmy sat down opposite her along with Detective Constable Tarret.

'Is the tape in?' asked Jimmy over her shoulder and Trul gave a sleepy 'Yes.'

To her amazement, Agatha heard herself being cautioned and then Jimmy's flat emotionless voice asking her if she wanted a lawyer.

'No,' said Agatha. 'I haven't done anything.'

'I have a report here that your fur coat was vandalized. In your preliminary statement, you said nothing about Mrs Juddle. So why did you go to see her in the middle of the night?'

Agatha's mind went this way and that. Then she decided that the truth was the only thing that would serve.

'I didn't tell the police I had been to Francie because I was ashamed to say I had been consulting the local witch.' Agatha unwound the scarf from her head and bent it forward. 'Some hairdresser shampooed my head with depilatory instead of shampoo and my hair didn't seem to be growing back properly. Mrs Daisy Jones at the hotel recommended Francie. I went along to her and bought a bottle of hair tonic. While I was there, she made several remarks about my coat.'

'Exactly what did she say?'

'I can't remember exactly. She said something about all the little animals that had been killed to make it and that I shouldn't be wearing it. I was upset after the coat had been vandalized. I thought I would go and wake her up and see if she had any red paint marks on her hands or under her nails. I knocked at the cottage door, hard. The door swung open. I went upstairs to look for the bedroom. I wanted to surprise her asleep. I wanted to look at her hands. But when I pushed open the bedroom door and turned on the light, I saw her the way you found her. I should have checked to see if she was still alive, but I couldn't bring myself to do that. I phoned for the police and ambulance and then went downstairs to wait. Look here,' said Agatha with some of her usual energy, 'if I'd bumped her off, I would simply have run away. My fingerprints are over everything.'

'So Mrs Juddle gave you hair restorer. Anything else?'

'No,' lied Agatha, thinking of that bottle of love potion which was still in her handbag, glad she had not left it in the hotel room for the police to find.

'So let's go back to the beginning again . . .'

Jimmy carefully took her through her story several times, obviously hoping she would slip up or come out with another bit of information.

At last, she was fingerprinted and told she was free to go but cautioned not to leave Wyckhadden.

A police car drove her the short distance to the hotel. She went up to her room and wearily opened the door. The room was in chaos. At first she thought she had been burgled until she realized there was fingerprint dust everywhere. Because of the murder, the forensic team had been sent in immediately. There was a knock at the door. She opened it to find the night porter standing there.

'I forgot to tell you,' he said, his eyes darting around the room, 'that the police took your fur coat away for evidence. Here's the receipt.'

'Thanks,' said Agatha.

'What's this about a murder?'

'Do you mind? I want to sleep.' Agatha shut the door in his face.

She was too tired to take a bath or shower. She creamed off her make-up, undressed and went to bed, but decided to sleep with the lights on in case darkness should bring back the horrors of the night too vividly.

Agatha was awakened early in the morning by the shrill sound of the telephone. It was a reporter from the *Hadderton Gazette*. 'Can't talk now,' she said and hung up. Then she phoned the switchboard and told them that no calls were to be put through to her room and then fell asleep again. She drifted in and out of sleep, vaguely aware that from time to time someone was knocking at her door.

At last she rose about noon and had just bathed and dressed when the phone rang. 'I told you not to put any calls through,' she snapped.

'Mrs Raisin? This is Inspector Jessop. I am downstairs and would like a few words with you.'

Agatha hung up, checked her make-up carefully and adjusted the blue scarf around her head, then went downstairs.

'We'll go into the lounge,' said Jimmy. 'It's empty at the moment.'

'No police sidekick?' said Agatha. 'Is this a friendly call?'

'Hardly.'

They walked into the lounge and sat down in huge armchairs by the long windows. On a coffee-table in front of them were spread the day's papers. 'Nothing in the press yet,' said Jimmy. 'Too late for them.'

'When did she die?' asked Agatha. 'I mean, the other residents will tell you I was in the hotel all evening.'

'We're waiting for the report. It is very hard to pinpoint the actual time of any death.'

'Have you found out how someone could have got into my room and slashed my coat?'

'No, it could have been a previous resident. We're checking the maids. Of course, there's a passkey. About last night, let's start again now you are rested. Why should you think a woman whom you had consulted about hair tonic should have slashed your coat, all because of a few off remarks?'

'I was rattled by the vandalism. I was furious. Oh, I may as well tell you the truth. I didn't like the way you went off me at that dance after I told you I was an amateur detective. I wanted to show you what I could do.'

'That's madness,' said Jimmy coldly. 'I wouldn't put it past you to bump off someone or slash your own coat. Women of your age who fancy themselves as amateur detectives will sometimes do anything to get publicity.'

'I do need a lawyer. If there was a witness to this conversation, I would sue you,' shouted Agatha.

'You must admit it looks odd. We had a murder in Wyckhadden twelve years ago and that's it. You arrive, and suddenly we have two incidents connected to you.'

'I am not a freak and I am not mad,' said Agatha in a thin voice. 'Did you come here for the sole purpose of insulting me?'

He passed a large hand over his face.

'I'm so tired I don't know what to think. But you're right. My remarks were unprofessional and out of order.' He leaned behind him and pressed a bell on the wall. 'I'll get us a drink.'

'I haven't had breakfast yet.'

The manager, Mr Martin, came bustling up. 'Inspector, the press are outside and are troubling our guests. Could you ask them to move on?'

Jimmy rose to his feet. 'I'll do what I can. Bring Mrs Raisin here a gin and tonic and me a half-pint of lager.'

'This has never happened to me before,' said Mr Martin crossly. He was a plump man in a tight suit with a high colour.

'I have never had a coat slashed before,' said Agatha crossly. 'Are we getting these drinks or not?'

The manager strode off, his fat shoulders stiff with disapproval.

Through the window, Agatha could see Jimmy talking to the press. A waiter came in with the drinks. Agatha suddenly realized that the police had made an oversight. They had not searched her handbag. If they had, they would have found that wretched love potion. She opened her handbag and took the small bottle out, planning to shove it down the side of the armchair and then recover it later. But a shaft of sunlight through the windows lit up the glass of lager Jimmy had ordered. Why not? thought Agatha. And I hope it poisons him. Probably only sugar and water. She looked around the empty lounge and then tipped half the bottle into the lager. Then she remembered Francie had said five drops. Agatha stared anxiously at the lager. It had turned a darker colour. She shoved the bottle down the side of the armchair.

Jimmy came back in, sat down, and took a hefty pull from his glass. 'There's no moving the press. But I tried.'

Agatha looked at him anxiously. 'Lager all right?'

'I suppose so,' said Jimmy. 'Funny sort of back taste, but there's all these odd foreign lagers around these days. Where was I?'

'You were insulting me,' said Agatha. 'You were saying I probably ripped up my own coat and then went out and killed Francie Juddle.'

'I'm sorry. I told you. Look, I'll tell you what got up my nose about you. No, I don't think you did it because as you say, you would hardly put your fingerprints over everything and then phone the police. The fact is . . . I told you about that other murder we had in Wyckhadden?'

'Yes.'

'It was a disaster. A woman in one of the old fishermen's cottages was found dead, beaten to death, quite savagely, an old woman. Her jewellery had gone and the contents of her purse. We suspected the grandson who had form, and we were closing in on him. He shared a flat with two other ne'er-do-wells in the council estate at the back of the town. But along comes this Miss Biddle, a local resident, spinster in her fifties. Had read every detective story ever published and fancied herself as the local Miss Marple. It was common enough gossip around the town about the grandson, everyone saying they were pretty sure he did it. So she decided to go and confront the grandson herself, lying to him, telling him she had proof positive he had done it. So he bashes *her* to death. We catch up with him in Brighton and get him on both counts. Miss Biddle used to waylay me on the street, bragging about how she had solved the case of the missing cat or had found someone else's lost handbag, so when you started up at the pier dance about all your adventures, I thought, oh God, we've got another one here.'

'If you check up with Mircester police, they can confirm my stories,' said Agatha frostily.

'I did phone Mircester police this morning and talked to a Detective Inspector Wilkes. He didn't exactly confirm your stories about being the great detective. The way he put it, it was more like you had a habit of blundering into things.'

'After all the help I've given them!' Agatha was outraged.

'Anyway, Agatha,' said Jimmy, suddenly smiling at her, 'keep out of this one.'

'As soon as you give me permission to leave this hell-hole, I'm going,' said Agatha. She picked up her gin and tonic and took a swallow and shuddered. 'Too early in the day for me.'

'It's two in the afternoon.'

'I've missed lunch.'

'Come on and I'll take you for a bite of something.'

Agatha stared at him. He was smiling again. Was there something in that love potion after all?

'I'll just go up and get my coat.'

Once in her room, Agatha unwound the scarf from her head, picked up the bottle of hair restorer and rubbed the lotion into the bald patches. If that love potion could make Jimmy smile at her again, then there might be something in the witch's products. Then she wound the scarf round her head again, put on her coat, and went downstairs.

'Aren't you supposed to avoid socializing with suspects?' she asked.

'I have a few hours off, and if anyone sees us, they'll only think I'm grilling you for more information.'

'Have you questioned the other residents of this hotel?'

'The police have been taking statements from them all morning.'

They went outside. The press clamoured to know if Agatha was being arrested.

'No,' said Jimmy curtly. 'And don't follow us or you'll get no more information out of me. And move away from the entrance of the hotel. I've already warned you.' But cameras clicked in Agatha's face and a television camera was shoved in her face. Head down, and taking Jimmy's arm, she walked with him along the promenade.

He turned up one of the side streets and led her to a small café. There was a NO SMOKING sign on the door. Agatha thought that perhaps she should have asked the witch for a cure for smoking.

They sat down at a table. Agatha picked up a small menu. The café specialized in 'light snacks'. She ordered quiche and salad and Jimmy ordered a pot of tea.

'So you were playing Scrabble with the other residents?' began Jimmy.

'Yes, I told you.'

'What are they like?'

'I haven't really got to know them that well. It was Daisy Jones who recommended Francie. She seems quite keen on Colonel Lyche, but he doesn't notice her. He seems pretty set in his ways. Then there's Jennifer Stobbs and Mary Dulsey and Harry Berry. What did we talk about? Well, Scrabble, letters, words. Nothing personal apart from "Would you like another drink, Mrs Raisin?"'

'Did any of them leave during the game?'

'Daisy Jones went to powder her nose but she used the downstairs loo. Colonel Lyche went to get drinks from the bar. So did Mr Berry. I don't suppose any of them have a horrible past.'

'We're digging into it. Francie Juddle kept an appointments book. They all consulted her.'

'Ah!' Agatha's eyes gleamed.

'Daisy Jones consulted her because she ran seances and Daisy wanted to get in touch with her late husband. The colonel has a liver complaint. Jennifer Stobbs asked for a love potion.'

'Who for? I mean, who was she going to use it on?'

'She insists it was for a friend. Mary Dulsey for warts, Harry Berry for rheumatism.'

'What a gullible lot!'

'You went to Francie yourself,' said Jimmy.

'Did she have me in her book?' asked Agatha.

'Yes, hair tonic.' Agatha heaved a sigh of relief. No mention of love potion.

'But apart from the residents at the hotel,' Jimmy was saying, 'an awful lot of the townspeople went to Francie.'

'Did she make a good living out of it?'

'Yes, I believe she was a wealthy woman, but we're checking with her solicitor to see how much she left.'

'What about family?'

'She has a daughter, Janine, who will probably inherit and who may take over the business.'

'It's probably her.'

'Doubtful. She visited her mother often and appeared very fond of her.'

'Is she married?'

'Yes, to a layabout called Cliff Juddle.'

'Juddle! Did she marry her cousin, or what?'

'Something like that. The Juddles are gypsies.'

'So couldn't this Cliff have bumped her off?'

'Anything's possible,' said Jimmy. 'But folk say that Janine is a very bossy woman, very tough. If Cliff killed the mother hoping to get his hands on the daughter's money, he wouldn't have much of a chance. Janine holds the purse-strings.'

'What does she do?'

'Same as her mother, but over in Hadderton. She may move here because the mother's was the more profitable business. There's a lot of old residents in Wyckhadden and the old have ailments and some of the older generation are superstitious. We raided a couple of her seances but could find nothing phoney, like muslin, or tapes, or thugs under the table to make it move. Mind you, these things do leak out and I always felt she had been forewarned.'

'But there must be trickery somewhere!'

'Oh, I'm sure there is but we were never able to find any.'

Agatha's quiche arrived. After she had eaten it she still felt hungry and looked longingly at the display of cakes.

'Like a cake?' asked Jimmy, following her gaze.

'Well . . .'

'I'll have one as well.'

'Oh, in that case . . .'

May as well make a good job of it, thought Agatha, ordering a slice of chocolate fudge cake. The menu boasted, 'We sell the best gateau cakes.' I wonder what the French tourists make of that one, thought Agatha.

The cake was delicious.

'So do I still have to stay in Wyckhadden?' asked Agatha.

'Yes, I'm afraid you do. And I forgot to tell you, my detective sergeant, Peter Carroll, will be on duty soon and he wants to ask you a few more questions. I'll walk you round to the police station when you're ready.'

'Aren't you coming?'

'I'm going home for a couple of hours' sleep. Ready to go?'

Detective Sergeant Peter Carroll was a thin-faced man with a courteous manner which belied his seemingly endless capacity for asking probing questions. Agatha described again the events of the previous night, although now the whole thing was beginning to seem unreal. The interview room had a high window through which sunlight shone. Dust motes floated in the sunbeams. The table at which Agatha sat was scarred and stained with the rings of many coffee cups and cigarette burns. The walls were painted that sour shade of lime green so beloved by bureaucracy in Britain.

Agatha was beginning to feel sleepy again.

'So we go back to the reason you left in the middle of the night to wake up a woman you just *thought* might have vandalized your coat. Why?' asked Carroll.

'I am by way of being an amateur detective,' said Agatha. Carroll consulted a fax on the papers in front of him and gave a brief cynical smile. Probably a fax from Wilkes telling them I'm an interfering busybody, thought Agatha. 'Since Mrs Juddle had criticized my wearing of the coat, I thought she might have had something to do with it. I thought if I paid her a surprise visit, she might still have traces of paint on her hands.'

There was a knock at the door and then it opened and Tarret's head appeared around it. 'A word, sir.'

'Excuse me.' Carroll went out. A policewoman seated in the corner by the tape machine stared stolidly ahead. Agatha stifled a yawn. Oh, to be home in Carsely in her own cottage with her cats. She had been silly to run away. She wondered if James thought of her.

Back in Carsely, James Lacey switched off the computer. He felt restless and bored. He had a dull feeling he refused to recognize that Carsely without Agatha was a lifeless sort of place. No one seemed to know where she had gone. The vicar's wife, Mrs Bloxby, probably knew but she wasn't telling anyone.

He decided to switch on the television and watch the teatime news. Another government scandal, another murder through road rage, and then the announcer said, 'Police in Wyckhadden are investigating the death of a local witch. Mrs Frances Juddle was found battered to death in her cottage. She was found by a visitor, a Mrs Agatha Raisin.' There was a still photograph of Agatha in a police car. 'Mrs Raisin from the village of Carsely in Gloucestershire is reported to be a friend of Inspector Jimmy Jessop, who is in charge of the case.' Film of Agatha leaving the hotel with Jimmy, then a long shot of Agatha and Jimmy walking along the promenade, arm in arm. The announcer then went on to describe Wyckhadden as a quiet seaside resort where a great many retired people stayed. Interviews with various neighbours of Francie Juddle, all expressing shock. James watched, bemused. Agatha had never mentioned Wyckhadden. And surely, if she had been friendly with a police inspector, she would have bragged about it.

He switched off the television and went out and along to the vicarage. Mrs Bloxby answered the door to him. 'Why, Mr Lacey! How nice. Come in. We don't see much of you these days.'

'I've been busy. What's this about Agatha?'

'She felt the need of a holiday.'

'I have just seen her on television.'

James told her about Agatha and the murder of the witch of Wyckhadden.

'Poor Mrs Raisin. Murder does seem to follow her around.'

'It said on the television news that Agatha was a friend of some police inspector.'

'I saw the television news. How shocking! Poor Mrs Raisin. But I never heard her mention anything about a police inspector.'

'But why Wyckhadden?'

'I may as well tell you,' said Mrs Bloxby, 'now that you know where she is. She didn't know anything about Wyckhadden. She just closed her eyes and stuck a pin in the map.'

'She might have told me where she was going.'

'Why?' asked Mrs Bloxby gently. 'You have not been close for quite a time.'

'But we're neighbours!'

'No doubt she'll tell us all about it when she returns. Tea?'

'No, I don't want any more of your filthy tea,' Agatha was saying to the policewoman. The sun had gone down. The interview room was cold.

The door opened and Carroll came in again. 'We got someone for cutting up your coat.'

'Who was it?' asked Agatha.

'It was that girl you told Tarret about, who attacked you on the prom. Her name's Carly

Broomhead. We picked her up. She still had traces of red paint on her hands. Her sister works, or rather worked, now, as a maid at Garden Hotel. She's been fired.'

'It *would* be someone like her,' said Agatha bitterly. 'I can sue her until I'm black in the face, but she'll never be able to pay for another coat.'

'At least we've got that out the way and know it's not connected with the murder.'

'Oh, isn't it? In my opinion, anyone who slashes a coat is quite capable of bashing someone's head in.'

'Just leave investigation to the police in future, Mrs Raisin. You're free to go but keep yourself available for further questioning.' He turned to the policewoman and said, 'Interview with Mrs Agatha Raisin finished at eighteen hundred hours. Switch off the tape, Josie, and leave us for a moment.'

When the policewoman had gone, Carroll leaned forward and said, 'Jimmy Jessop's a decent man.'

'I am sure he is,' said Agatha stiffly.

'He was shattered by the death of his wife. I don't want him getting hurt or mucked about by the likes of you, see?'

'Why don't you concentrate on police work and mind your own damned business,' said Agatha, standing up.

'I am concentrating on police business and I

don't like the way you went out at one in the morning and found that body.'

'Are you charging me?'

'Not yet.'

'Then get stuffed.'

Agatha stormed out. As she hurried back to the hotel, she realized with a little shock that she had not had a cigarette that day. She opened her handbag and took out a packet of Benson & Hedges. Then she took a deep breath of fresh air and put them back. She was free of the stuff at last.

When she got back to the hotel, she was relieved to see that no press were waiting outside. The manager, Mr Martin, was waiting for her. 'If you would just step into the office, Mrs Raisin.'

She followed him into an office off the entrance hall.

'I am very distressed that a member, or rather, a former member, of my staff should have been party to the destruction of your coat, Mrs Raisin. We will not be charging you for your stay here.'

'Thank you,' said Agatha. 'I plan to make it as short as possible.'

'Our offer does not cover drinks,' he said awkwardly.

'I'll remember that,' said Agatha drily. Then she remembered the bottle of love potion she had thrust down the cushions of the armchair in the lounge. She was all at once anxious to retrieve it. 'Thank you.' She got to her feet and went out.

The colonel was reading a newspaper in the lounge and sitting in the armchair on which Agatha had sat earlier. Daisy Jones was sitting opposite him, knitting.

'What are you doing?' cried Daisy shrilly as Agatha plunged her hand down the side of the armchair on which the colonel was sitting.

'I left my medicine,' said Agatha, retrieving the bottle, although she was tempted to shock Daisy by saying, 'Just having a feel.'

'These are distressing times,' said the colonel. 'We are going to play Scrabble tonight as usual, all the same. Do join us.'

'Thank you.'

Why not, thought Agatha. Murder and mayhem may have arrived in Wyckhadden but the Scrabble game goes on.

Chapter Three

Agatha rubbed some more lotion into her bald patches before winding a chiffon scarf around her head and then went downstairs for dinner. After calling out 'Good evening' to the others, she picked up a paperback and began to read to ward them off. She would see enough of them over the Scrabble game.

The meal was roast pork, roast potatoes, apple sauce, and various vegetables. It had been preceded by Scotch broth and rolls and butter and was followed by meringues and ice cream. I shouldn't even be eating half of this, thought Agatha, but what the hell, it's been a bad time and I need some comfort.

But the heavy meal had the effect of making her feel sleepy again. Only ambition to find out something about these other residents forced her into joining their Scrabble game.

She refused the offer of a drink from the colonel. Mary Dulsey shook out the Scrabble tiles and old Harry put on a pair of gold-rimmed glasses and laid out pen and notebook to log the scores.

'It's nice the weather has cleared up,' said Daisy brightly. 'Oh, thank you, Colonel,' to that gentleman, who had returned with a tray of drinks.

'Aren't we going to discuss the murder?' asked Agatha.

'But it's our Scrabble game,' said Jennifer.

The others were carefully sorting their tiles in rows. 'I don't know what I'm supposed to do with this lot,' grumbled Mary.

'They found out who vandalized my coat,' said Agatha.

'We know,' said the colonel. 'Mr Martin told us. Agatha, you have the highest tile. You start.'

Agatha looked at her letters. She leaned over the board and put down HOG. 'You have a T there and a U and another H,' reproved Daisy. 'You could have put THOUGH.'

'No helping,' barked the colonel, and Daisy blushed and whispered, 'Sorry.'

Agatha looked round the bent old heads in amazement. Why weren't they talking about the murder? But they had all been interviewed that morning, had probably discussed it among themselves, and now all they wanted was their usual game of Scrabble. Perhaps the best thing would be to try to tackle them one by one on the following day.

When the first game finished, she excused herself, saying she was tired, and went up to her room.

Again she slept with the light on.

In the morning, she went down for breakfast and approached Daisy Jones. 'Mind if I join you?'

Daisy cast a longing look at the colonel but he was barricaded behind the *Daily Telegraph*. 'Yes, do,' she said with obvious reluctance.

'Do you know I was the one who found poor Francie Juddle?' started Agatha.

'Yes, it was in the newspapers this morning.'

'What did you go to her for?'

Daisy looked uncomfortable. Then she said, 'Francie gave seances. She said she could get me in touch with my dead husband.'

'And did she?'

'Yes. I mean it was scary to hear Hugh's voice.'

'No trickery?'

'I suppose there must have been. I don't want to talk about it.'

'But –'

'No, I really don't want to talk about it. There are things one shouldn't dabble in.'

'I just wonder,' said Agatha slowly, 'if she knew your late husband. I mean did he come to Wyckhadden with you when he was alive?'

'Yes, we came every summer.' Daisy sighed.

'I suppose that's why I decided to retire here. So many happy memories. But Francie never met my Hugh. Let's talk about something else. What about you and the inspector?'

'I met him for the first time this week,' said Agatha. 'He took me to a dance on the pier.'

'What was that like?' asked Daisy wistfully. 'Is it still the same?'

'I suppose it is.'

'Hugh and I used to go to the dances there. I tried to get the colonel to take me, but he said he had no time for such nonsense.'

She looked so sad that Agatha said impulsively, 'We can always go together one evening. I mean you and me.'

'Oh, you are good.'

'It seems as if I'm stuck here for a bit. May as well.'

Daisy gave a surprisingly youthful giggle. 'I wonder what they'll do without me at their Scrabble game?'

They ate a companionable breakfast.

'I think I'll go for a walk,' said Agatha.

'When should we go to the dance?' asked Daisy eagerly. 'There's one on tonight.'

'May as well go then,' said Agatha, but already regretting her impulse.

Agatha went upstairs to get her coat. She decided to wash and blow-dry her hair before she went out and then apply some more of that lotion. She shampooed her hair and then examined her scalp. On the bald patches was now growing a faint fuzz of new hair. It's a miracle, thought Agatha. When I get back to Carsely, I'll get this hair lotion analysed and I might be able to make a fortune if it really works.

Feeling quite elated, she wound a pretty chiffon scarf around her head in a sort of Turkish turban, put on her coat and headed out of the hotel. It was very cold and windy, but Agatha was determined to exercise and return to Carsely a new, thin Agatha. She set out in the opposite direction she had gone before, to the east rather than the west. She kept away from the sea-wall, for the tide was high and occasionally a great wave would break over the wall. The air was full of the sounds of screaming sea-gulls and crashing sea. Reaching the end of the promenade in that direction, she turned back and headed west, past the hotel. She turned up into the centre of the town where she found an elegant little boutique. In the window was a short black silk chiffon dress, cut low and with thin straps. Bit chilly for Wyckhadden in winter, thought Agatha. But she knew she still had smooth shoulders and a good bust. Wouldn't do any harm to try it on.

She emerged twenty minutes later with the dress in a bag. It was too good for the pier dance, but for a candle-lit dinner with James Lacey . . .

Agatha found her steps leading her to that pub where she had first met Jimmy. It was just about lunch-time and he might be there.

She pushed opened the door of the pub and went in. It smelt like all dingy pubs, of stale beer and Bisto gravy.

No Jimmy. A couple of business men at one table, the adulterous couple at another, three youths propping up the bar.

She went over to the bar and ordered a gin and tonic. She took out her wallet to pay for it when a voice behind her said to the bartender, 'I'll get that, Charlie. And half a pint of lager for me.' She turned quickly and saw Jimmy smiling down at her.

'Thank you,' said Agatha. 'How are things going?'

He paid for the drinks and then they sat down at a table. 'The motive seems to have been robbery,' said Jimmy.

'Oh.' Agatha was disappointed. She had been nursing a dream where it would turn out one of the residents at the Garden had committed the murder and she would solve it.

'Her daughter, Janine, says she kept a large amount of cash in a padlocked metal box. The box was found this morning on the beach where it had been thrown. It was empty.'

'Forced?'

'No. Her keys were missing as well. Janine said she kept a key to the box with her car keys.'

'So it was not just some ordinary burglary. I mean, it wasn't some lout off the street. Someone knew where she kept the money.'

'Looks that way.'

'Any sign of what struck her?'

'Some sort of poker or cosh or bottle. Forensic are still working on that. Been shopping?'

'I found a pretty dress in a boutique in the town. I think it's too good to wear tonight, however.'

'What's happening tonight?'

'I'm going with Daisy Jones from the hotel to the pier dance.'

'Good for you.'

'I wish I'd never agreed to it,' said Agatha gloomily.

'We haven't ruled out that it might be one of them at the hotel, although it seems far-fetched.'

'The colonel's very fit,' said Agatha. 'Come to think of it, apart from old Mr Berry, they're all pretty fit.'

'Find out anything about them and Francie Juddle?'

'Only from Daisy Jones so far. She says she went to Francie to get in touch with her dead husband.' Agatha leaned forward, her eyes gleaming with excitement. 'Here's a strange thing. She said that the voice she heard at the seance sounded like that of her dead husband, Hugh, but she said Francie never knew Hugh.'

'She did, you know. She logged everything in her yearly appointments books and kept them all. We've got police going through them. Hugh Jones did go to her.'

'What for?'

'A cure for impotence.'

'So she *would* know what he sounded like!' said Agatha.

'By all accounts, our Francie was a great mimic.'

'But a man's voice!'

'She could have had an accomplice. We're going on *Crime Watch* tonight to appeal to people who consulted her to come forward.'

'What did old Mr Berry go to her for? Oh, you said it was rheumatism.'

'He also wanted to get in touch with his dead wife.'

'It's a cruel business, that,' said Agatha, 'conning people that way.'

'Oh, there are a lot of believers. They can't let go of the dead.'

'Did you ever feel that way . . . about your wife?'

'No, you see much as I missed her dreadfully, I didn't and I don't believe in seances. From my experience, people have to mourn and get it over with or they can go crazy. There's a lot to be said for a good old Irish wake.'

'No hope of you being at the dance tonight, Jimmy?'

He rubbed a weary hand over his face. 'I'm working flat out. I only nipped in here –' he flushed slightly – 'well, just for a break. I've got to be going.'

That love potion must really work, thought Agatha. She knew he had meant that he had come to the pub in the hope of seeing her.

'I'll walk with you,' said Agatha.

'I don't think that's wise,' said Jimmy awkwardly. 'You're still a suspect and I got a bit of a rocket from the force crime officer over at Hadderton when he saw us both on television. They're digging up a lot of colourful stuff out of your past, Agatha. I mean your husband being murdered, and all.'

'Oh, God.'

'Who's this chap, Lacey, you were thinking of marrying?'

'Just someone. I mean, it didn't work out.'

'Not still carrying a torch for him?'

Agatha stared at the table. 'No.'

'Good.' He patted her hand.

Agatha sat smiling to herself after he had left. She liked his thick white skin and his sleepy eyelids and his tall figure. What would it be like being married to a police inspector? She began to imagine their wedding, but when she got to the bit where James Lacey asked for a dance with the bride and told her he had always loved her Agatha snapped out of it. It would be typical of such as James Lacey to tell her he loved her when there was no chance of doing anything about it.

She left the pub and bought the newspapers and then went to the café she had gone to with Jimmy for lunch, not wanting to return to the hotel for one of their mammoth meals.

She sat and read the newspapers. On the front of two of them was a photograph of Janine Juddle. In an interview, she said she would be moving to Wyckhadden to carry on her mother's business of helping people. She said she would ask the spirits of the dead to rise up and find the murderer of her poor mother. Janine was a hard-faced blonde. Beside her in the photograph was a surly-looking man with close-cropped hair. The husband. Now he could have done it, thought Agatha. Janine might hold the purse-strings, but ready money had been stolen and who better to know that it had been there than the son-in-law.

Agatha wondered how long it would be before Janine started her business in Wyckhadden.

She went for another long walk and then back to the hotel. She felt she ought to go into the lounge and see if she could grill any of the residents, but she was suddenly very tired. She would see enough of them later.

Agatha went down for dinner wearing a red satin blouse and a long evening skirt. She had tried on the little black dress but decided again that such glamour was definitely wasted on Wyckhadden.

Daisy Jones was resplendent in an evening gown of pink net covered with sequins. When had she last seen a gown like that? wondered

Agatha. The fifties. But it was the sight of the others that made Agatha blink. Old Mr Berry was wearing a greenish-black evening suit and the colonel was also in evening dress and black tie. Jennifer Stobbs was wearing a black velvet trouser suit and Mary Dulsey was exposing a lot of wrinkled skin in a strapless green silk gown.

'We're all going,' Daisy shouted over. 'Isn't this *fun*?'

Just what I need, thought Agatha bitterly. A night out with a bunch of wrinklies. That was the awful thing about socializing with the old. You could no longer keep up the pretence that you were young and dashing any more. Let me see, thought Agatha gloomily. I'm in my fifties; Daisy, about mid-sixties; Mary and Jennifer the same; the colonel, oh, about seventy-odd; and Mr Berry, definitely in the seventies. And the way time rushes by these days, it won't be long before I'm one of them and the tragedy is that I'll still feel about twenty-five.

But after dinner, as they all set out together into a calm frosty night, Agatha felt her spirits rising. They were all like excited teenagers. But their spirits were dampened as they walked along the pier past the closed shops and amusement arcades to come up against a poster advertising that it was disco night. Young people were already walking along the pier in the direction of the dance hall.

'Dear me,' said Daisy in a little voice. 'I

suppose we may as well all have a drink and just watch. But I did so want to dance.'

They left their coats and, crowding together, they walked into the ballroom and gathered round a table at the dance floor. The colonel took their orders for drinks and went off to the bar.

'They look like a lot of savages,' growled Jennifer. She really should shave that moustache, thought Agatha impatiently. No reason to let herself go like that. She did not feel exactly glamorous herself with her hair tucked up under a red scarf to match her blouse. She had arranged it in the Turkish-turban style but she still felt like an old frump. The colonel returned bearing a tray with their drinks.

'This isn't a good idea,' whimpered Mary. 'I can hardly hear myself think.'

A group of youths were sniggering and staring at them from the other side of the floor. Then one, a tall youth in a leather jacket and jeans, detached himself from the group. He walked over to their table and then, turning, winked at his friends, and said to Agatha, 'Want to dance, sweetheart?'

Dammit, I will not be old before my time, thought Agatha rebelliously.

'Sure,' she said, getting up on the floor.

Agatha was a good disco dancer. Her long black skirt had a long slit up the side which opened as she danced, showing the world that Agatha Raisin had a smashing pair of legs. She gave herself up to the jungle beat of the music, forgetting that this young punk had only asked her for a joke, although he was a superb dancer. She was dimly aware that people were cheering, that people were clearing a space around them.

When the dance finished, Agatha returned to the table, flushed and happy.

'I don't know how you do it,' marvelled the colonel.

'Come on and I'll show you,' teased Agatha, not for a minute expecting him to take her up on her offer.

'I would be honoured,' said the colonel formally.

As the colonel started to throw himself about, hands waving, legs kicking with abandon, Agatha was reminded of James. James danced like that. At one point, she looked over the colonel's shoulder and saw with glad amazement that Daisy and Harry Berry had joined the dancers, as had Mary and Jennifer.

After that, various young people asked them to dance. They were no longer oddities. They were regarded as fun, and Agatha thought it was amazing that young people with nose-rings and spiky hair and terrifying clothes, when you got to know them, mostly always turned out to be nice and ordinary.

They stuck it out gamely to the last dance. 'Well, I'm blessed,' said the colonel as they walked along the pier. 'I can't remember when I've enjoyed myself so much in ages.'

Highly elated, old Harry was performing dance steps along the pier. Daisy caught Agatha's arm. 'Could I have a quiet word with you when we get back?'

'Sure,' said Agatha, stifling a yawn. 'But not too long. I'm beat. Come up to my room.'

In Agatha's room, Daisy looked at her pleadingly. 'I was jealous of you tonight, Agatha.'

'Oh, why?' Agatha unwound her turban and peered at her scalp. By all that was holy, her hair was growing.

'Well, the colonel paid you a lot of attention.'

'You're keen on the colonel?'

'Yes, very.'

'But what can I do?' asked Agatha. 'He's not keen on me, I can tell you that. He just wanted a bit of fun.'

'My clothes are very old-fashioned. I realized that tonight. And my hair. I wondered if you could go shopping with me tomorrow and sort of *make me over*.'

'Gladly,' said Agatha. 'We'll set out after breakfast. It'll be fun.'

And so it will, she thought in surprise. Agatha had run her own successful public relations firm but had taken early retirement. But taking someone in hand and improving their image had been part of her job. Life had suddenly acquired colour and meaning again. And what was more, she hadn't had a cigarette. She took a full packet out of her handbag, opened it, broke up all the cigarettes and threw them in the waste bin.

In the morning, after breakfast, Agatha found that Mary and Jennifer wanted to join the shopping expedition. She led them through to the lounge. 'We'd better prepare a plan of action first,' she said. 'Are you game?'

They all nodded. 'Well, for a start, you've all got old-fashioned hair-styles,' said Agatha, 'but fortunately you all seem to have strong, healthy hair that will take tinting. I think I need to start off with taking you all to a good hairdresser and getting you all styled. Then a beautician. Face and skin are important.'

'You can't do anything about wrinkles,' said Jennifer.

'Oh, yes, you can,' said Agatha, 'and I'm not talking face-lift. Do you know of a good hairdresser? I mean, one you haven't gone to?'

'We all just go to Sally's in the High Street.'

'I'll ask the manager.' Agatha went through to the office. Mr Martin listened to her request and said, 'There's a retired couple in Wyckhadden. He was a hairdresser and she was a beautician. They still do some work privately.'

'I don't know . . .' began Agatha doubtfully.

'He used to be Jerome of Bond Street.'

'Good heavens,' said Agatha faintly. 'I forget how old I am myself. I used to go to Jerome. He was very good. Can you give me his number?'

Supplied with the number, Agatha phoned up. Jerome was delighted to hear from her. She could bring her ladies along and he and his wife would get to work.

In all her crusading zeal, Agatha had quite forgotten about the murder. By the end of the morning, Daisy's hair was a shining honey-blonde and her wrinkles had been smoothed out with a collagen treatment. Jennifer had a short smart bob and her moustache had been removed and her eyebrows shaped. Mary had a pretty arrangement of soft curls and a smoother face.

Chattering happily, they all had lunch in a restaurant on the promenade and then Agatha led them round the shops. 'I hope you all can afford this,' she said guiltily.

They all said yes, they could. Agatha's mind returned to murder. Jennifer had paid for all her purchases from a wallet bulging with cash while the rest used credit cards, and Jennifer was a powerful woman. And as her mind returned to thoughts of murder, so did the craving for a cigarette return with force. 'No, not pink, Daisy,' she said as Daisy held up a blouse for her inspection. 'Blue, maybe. And you need a different size of bra.'

'What's wrong with the one I've got on?'

'It's too tight. It's giving you bulges where you shouldn't have bulges.'

I mean it's not as if I gave up smoking, Agatha argued with herself. It gave me up, so to speak. I didn't sign the pledge. Just one puff would be heaven. Well, maybe later.

'Somehow the idea of Scrabble seems a bit flat,' said Jennifer in her deep voice. 'But I suppose that's all we've got on the cards tonight.'

But when they returned to the hotel, it was to find that the colonel had taken the liberty of booking seats for them all at a production of Gilbert and Sullivan's *Mikado* and had arranged an early dinner.

This is like a girls' dormitory, thought Agatha in amusement as Daisy and Mary and Jennifer called in at her room to ask her to vet what they were wearing.

They all went downstairs together. 'By George, ladies, you've youthed,' said old Harry, his eyes twinkling.

'That blue suits you, Daisy,' said the colonel, 'and your hair's pretty.' Daisy's eyes shone and she squeezed Agatha's arm.

The theatre was an old-fashioned one bedecked with plaster gilt cherubs and a large chandelier.

The colonel, who had been carrying a large box of chocolates, passed it along, and there was much fumbling for spectacles as they tried to read the chart of flavours.

Agatha had never seen a Gilbert and Sullivan operetta and feared it would all prove to be a bit arty-farty, but from the overture on, she was riveted. In that evening, for a brief time, she became the child she had never really been. It was a novelty to her to have the capacity of sheer enjoyment. Pleasure for Agatha had always been bitter-sweet, always had a this-won't-last feeling. But that evening, the glory of escapism and warmth and security seemed to go on forever.

As they filed out after the performance, the colonel could be heard saying to Daisy, 'The Lord High Executioner could have been better,' but Agatha could find no fault with anything.

They went to a nearby pub for drinks. The colonel told an amusing story about a Gilbert and Sullivan performance in the army. Jennifer made them laugh by saying she had once played Buttercup in *Pirates of Penzance* and had forgotten all the words and so had tried to make them up.

It was only when Agatha was undressing for bed that she suddenly thought it curious that not one of them had mentioned the murder, or was curious about the murder. Maybe they considered it bad form. Maybe their elderly brains had already forgotten about the whole thing.

But in the following week, as she went out with her new-found friends, she, too, discovered that, for the first time, she wasn't much interested in finding out who had murdered Francie, largely because she was convinced the culprit was the son-in-law and the police with the aid of forensic would soon arrest him. And Jimmy had not called, not once.

James Lacey was shopping in Mircester when he ran into Detective Sergeant Bill Wong. Bill was looking round and chubby, a sure sign he had no love in his life. When Bill was smitten by some girl, he always slimmed down.

'I see Agatha's got herself involved in another murder,' said Bill. 'Heard from her?'

'No,' said James. 'Have you?'

'Not a word. I thought she would have been on the phone asking me to help. Why don't you go down there and see her?'

'I can't manage it. I'm thinking of going abroad again. Friends of mine have a villa in Greece and they've invited me over.'

Poor Agatha, thought Bill. James was hardly the impassioned lover.

When he got back to police headquarters, he got a telephone call from the baronet, Sir Charles Fraith. 'What's our Aggie been up to?' demanded Charles.

'I only know what I've read in the papers,' said Bill. 'Then I gather Wyckhadden police have been checking up on her background.'

'If you're speaking to her, give her my love.'

'Why don't you go and see her?'

'Shooting season. Got a big house party. Can't get away.'

Poor Agatha, thought Bill again. I hope she isn't too lonely.

Agatha was taking a brisk walk along the pier ten days after the murder when she saw the tall, slim figure of the colonel in front of her and quickened her steps to catch up with him.

'Fine morning,' said Agatha. It had turned quite mild for mid-winter, one of those milky grey days when all colour seemed to have been bleached out of the sea and the sky, and even the sea-gulls were silent.

'Morning, Agatha,' said the colonel. 'All set for the dance tonight? More our style.'

He pointed to a poster advertising OLD-TYME DANCING. 'Yes, we've all got new gowns to dazzle you,' said Agatha. 'Colonel, why do none of you ever talk about that dreadful murder?'

'Not the sort of thing one talks about,' said the colonel. 'Nasty business. Best forgotten.'

'You went to Francie, didn't you?'

'My liver had been playing up and my quack couldn't seem to come up with anything sensible. Kept telling me to stop drinking. May as well be dead in that case. Went to Francie. She gave me some powders. Haven't had any trouble since.'

Agatha thought that as the colonel did not drink very much, and had probably received a bad health scare to slow down his drinking, it was probably due to that rather than Francie's powders that he hadn't had any more trouble.

'What did you make of her? Francie, I mean.'

'All right. I'd expected a lot of mumbo-jumbo. But she seemed a sensible sort of woman. I'm surprised her daughter's moved in and set up in business so quickly.'

'She has?'

'Yes, there was a small ad in the local paper this morning.'

Agatha's detective curiosity was roused again. 'That is odd.'

'I don't think it's odd,' said the colonel. 'Tasteless, maybe. I think she's cashing in on the publicity about her mother's death.'

'I wonder if people will go to her,' mused Agatha.

'Bound to. There was also a bit in the local paper about Francie's cures, saying there was a lot to be said for old-fashioned herbal medicine.'

'That's what she used? Herbs?'

'Or grass.'

'Grass?'

'Grass. Pot. Hash. We had a lady who was resident at the Garden – she's dead now, poor old thing. She was subject to fits of depression and so she went to Francie, who gave her something. Well, after that, whenever she had taken some of what Francie had prescribed, she used to get all giggly and silly. I've seen the effects of pot and I thought Francie had given her something with hash in it.'

'Didn't you report it?'

'Old lady had terminal cancer. I thought, if it keeps her happy, so be it.'

'And yet you went to her yourself?'

'She seemed to be all right generally. Mary was plagued with warts and she cured those, things like that. I had high blood pressure once, everything seemed to outrage me – politics, modern youth, you name it. I went on a diet and decided not to worry about anything, interfere in anything, just look after myself. Worked a treat. That's why I let things like this murder alone.'

'Did you know Daisy's husband?'

'Met him once. Gloomy sort of fellow.'

'What did he die of?'

'Lung cancer. Sixty-cigarettes-a-day man.'

Agatha, who had been fighting with the craving for a cigarette, felt the longing for one sharply increase. Odd that the minute she heard something awful about the effects of cigarettes, the longing for one should hit her. Maybe that's why the cigarette manufacturers didn't balk at putting grim warnings on cigarette packets. They probably knew that at the heart of every addict, there's a death wish.

'You've done wonders with the ladies' appearance.' The colonel strolled on with Agatha at his side. He seemed happy to change the subject. 'Daisy's looking really pretty.'

'Thinking of getting married?' teased Agatha.

'What me? By George, no! Once was enough.'

'Wasn't it happy?'

'Wonder if those chaps have caught any fish?' The colonel waved his stick at men fishing at the end of the pier. So the subject of his marriage was closed.

As they turned back and walked towards the hotel, Agatha stumbled and he tucked her arm in his. 'Better hang on to me,' he said. 'Don't want you twisting an ankle before this evening. You should wear flats.'

'I always like a bit of a heel,' said Agatha. She looked towards the hotel. There was a flash at one of the windows. Could be binoculars, thought Agatha. I wonder whose room that is.

When they went into the warmth of the hotel, to the Victorian hush of the Garden with its thick carpets, thick curtains and solid walls, Agatha felt all her old restlessness coming back. She went up to her room and unwound the scarf from her head. There was not enough hair covering the hitherto bald patches. She shook the bottle. Only a little left.

She could kill two birds with one stone. She could go along and have a look at this Janine and see what she was like and also see if she had any of her mother's hair lotion left. She didn't want to use up the last little bit in case it turned out that Janine didn't have any and that last bit must be kept for analyses.

She brushed her hair and decided there was no longer any reason to wear a scarf.

Agatha called in at the dining-room on her way out to tell the others she would be skipping lunch. The waistband of her skirt felt comfortably loose for the first time in months and she did not want to sabotage her figure with one of the hotel's massive lunches.

'Where are you going?' asked Mary.

'I'm going to see Francie Juddle's daughter.'

They all stared at her. 'Why?' asked Jennifer.

'It's my hair. Remember I had these bald patches? Francie gave me some hair tonic and it worked a treat. I'm going to see if she has any of her mother's stuff left.'

Agatha turned away and said over her shoulder, 'If she's such a witch, she may even be able to rouse the spirits of the dead to tell me who murdered her mother.'

There was a sudden stillness behind her, but she went on her way. They probably all thought her visit was bad form.

Chapter Four

Agatha felt quite excited as she made her way along the promenade to Partons Lane.

At the cottage, a surly-looking young man answered the door. 'You got an appointment?' he demanded.

'No.'

'Well, you'll need to come back. Two o'clock's the first free appointment.'

'Put my name down,' said Agatha. 'Agatha Raisin.'

'Right you are.'

'You won't forget?'

'Naw.'

So that's that for the moment, Agatha thought. She made her way to the pub where she had first met Jimmy. To her surprise and delight, he was sitting at a table with a half-finished glass of lager in front of him.

'Agatha!' He rose to his feet. 'Sit down and I'll get you something. The usual?'

'Thanks, Jimmy.'

Jimmy returned with her drink. 'So how are things?' he asked.

'I've been jauntering around with the people from the hotel. We're going to the dance tonight. Have they found out when the murder was committed?'

'Can't ever be exact. She hadn't had any supper. Nothing in her stomach to indicate she'd eaten anything since lunchtime. The pathologist thinks it might have been between five and six o'clock, going by rigor mortis and all that sort of business.'

'Oh, but that means it could have been done by one of them at the hotel. Surely the neighbours saw who went in and out?'

'There's the problem. The cottages on either side and across the road are weekend cottages. And the only permanent resident four doors away is nearly blind.'

'But someone carrying a cash box and emptying out the contents and throwing it over the sea-wall would surely be noticed?'

'Not really. Have you been around Wyckhadden at six o'clock? It's the ideal time for a murder. All the shops and offices are closed and everyone indoors having their tea. Only the really posh still have dinner in the evening down here. The murderer could have transferred the money into coat pockets and then just have dropped the empty box over the wall. It was high tide and the sea would have been up.'

'But the appointments book. Was anyone booked in for six?'

'She always took the last appointment at four-thirty. That was a Mrs Derwent, who took her little boy along who's got trouble with asthma.'

'What about the weapon? Surely that would have been dropped over the sea-wall with the box?'

'Maybe. But there's everything down there at low tide that could have been used – empty bottles, iron bars, bits of wood. The sea's rough and the pebbles would have scoured any evidence clean away.'

'So are you looking for anyone?'

'We suspected Janine's husband, Cliff. But he has a cast-iron alibi. He was playing bowls from early afternoon to late evening at the bowling alley over at Hadderton. Masses of witnesses.'

'Rats.'

'As you say, rats. Don't worry about it, Agatha. At least your lot at the hotel seem to be in the clear.'

'Why?'

'It's a young man's murder. I'm sure of that. That blow that killed her was done with one brutal bashing to the head.'

'They're pretty spry, and Jennifer Stobbs, for example, is still a powerful woman.'

'It's usually someone with a bit of form, and they're all respectable people who don't need the cash. It takes a lot of money to pay the Garden's prices, year in, year out. Your hair's grown back in. Very nice.'

'I wonder if it was that lotion I got from Francie.'

'I think it would probably have grown back in anyway. I'll need to go.'

'We're all going to the pier dance tonight,' said Agatha hopefully.

'If I find a spare minute, I'll drop in. But don't waste time worrying about who did the murder. If you ask me, it could have been anyone. She had so many clients over the years and one of them could have seen her putting money away in that box and talked about it at home. Some youth hears about it and tells his pals. I've a nasty feeling this one isn't going to be solved.'

Agatha walked back to Partons Lane. Again the young man answered the door. 'Are you Cliff? Janine's husband?' asked Agatha.

'Yes.' He led her into the living-room and said, 'Wait there.'

The white cat was lying on the hearth. It saw Agatha and bared its pointed teeth in a hiss. Agatha eyed it warily in case it flew at her again.

Janine came in. She had dyed blonde hair piled up on top of her head. She had hard pale blue eyes fringed with white lashes, a thin, long nose and that L-shaped jaw which used to be regarded as a thing of beauty in Hollywood actresses of the eighties.

'What can I do for you?' she asked, smiling. The smile was not reflected in her hard, assessing eyes. Agatha felt that every item she was wearing had been priced.

'Your mother – excuse me, my condolences on your sad loss – sold me some hair tonic. I wonder if you have any left.'

'No, I'm sorry. I threw a lot of that stuff out. I don't deal so much in potions. I have seances, palm-reading, tarot, things like that. I could read your palm.'

'How much?'

'Ten pounds.'

Pretty steep, thought Agatha, but she was anxious to ingratiate herself with Janine.

'All right.'

'Give me your hands.'

Agatha held out her hands. 'You have a strong character,' said Janine. 'Like getting your own way.'

'I don't need a character assessment,' said Agatha testily.

'You have suffered a bereavement recently, a violent bereavement.' Agatha's husband's murder had been in all the papers. 'There are now three men in your life. Each loves you in his own way, but you will never marry again. There has been a great deal of danger in your life up until now, but that is all gone. You will now lead a quiet life until you die. Nor will you have sex with anyone from now on.'

'How can you tell all that?' Agatha was feeling angry.

'There is an affinity between us. You found my mother. There is a psychic bond between us. That is all.'

What a rotten ten pounds' worth, thought Agatha, and then was about to say something when she was hit by an idea.

'You said you do seances,' she said.

'Yes, I call up the spirits of the dead.'

'So who does your mother say murdered her?'

'It is too early. Any day now. She is getting established on the other side.'

Can't be unpacking anyway, thought Agatha sourly.

'Look, there's six of us along at the Garden Hotel. Would you consider doing a seance for us if the others are agreeable?'

'Certainly.'

'At the hotel?'

'No, I always do seances here.'

I'll bet you do, thought Agatha. Too many tricks to carry along.

She said aloud, 'I'll check with the others and let you know.'

She paid over ten pounds. 'How much do you charge for a seance?'

'Two hundred pounds.'

'Blimey.'

'It takes a lot out of me.'

And a lot out of everyone else's pocket, thought Agatha as she stumped along the promenade some minutes later.

When she arrived at the hotel, she took a look in the lounge. Mary was on her own by the fire, knitting. Agatha decided to join her. Mary rarely said anything. Jennifer always acted as spokeswoman for both of them.

Taking off her coat, Agatha sat down opposite her. Mary gave her a brief smile and went on knitting. She must have been quite pretty once, in a weak, rabbity sort of way, thought Agatha.

'I went to see Janine,' said Agatha.

'Francie's daughter? What was she like?'

'Read my palm at great expense and talked a lot of bollocks. Still, it might be a hoot if we all went along to one of her seances.'

'Do you think those things are real?'

'I can't see how. But it might be fun. She charges two hundred pounds, would you believe? Still, split up amongst six of us, it isn't too bad.'

'I wonder if she can tell about the living? I mean, if her spirits can tell about the living.'

'I doubt if she can any more than I can bring myself to believe she talks to the dead. Why the living?'

'Just someone I was keen on a long time ago.'

'A man?' asked Agatha, who often wondered whether Mary was in a relationship with Jennifer.

'Of course, a man. I often wonder where he is and what he is doing.'

'Didn't it work out?' asked Agatha sympathetically, thinking of James Lacey.

'It all went wrong.' Mary's large brown eyes filled with memories. 'But for a while, we were so happy. I was on holiday with my parents here, in Wyckhadden, and it was at this very hotel that I met him.'

'How old were you?'

'Twenty-two,' said Mary on a sigh. 'A long time ago. We got friendly, we walked on the beach, we went to dances.'

'Did you have an affair?'

Mary looked shocked. 'Oh, nothing like that. I mean, one didn't . . . *then*.'

'And so how did it end?'

'I gave him my address. I was living in Cirencester then with my parents. He lived in London. I waited but he didn't write. He hadn't given me a phone number, but I had his address. At last I couldn't bear it any longer. I went up to London, to the address he had given me. It was a rooming-house. The people there had never heard of him.'

'Maybe he gave you a false name?'

'It was his real name, the one he gave me, because he had a car. He had just passed his driving test and was very proud of his new licence. It had his name on it, Joseph Brady. I described what he looked like and I even had a photo with me, but the people in the rooming-house said he had never lived there and one lady had been there for the past ten years! He had said he was an advertising copy-writer. When I got home, I phoned all the advertising agencies that were listed. I went off sick from work to do it. Nobody had heard of him. I couldn't get over him. I went back to Wyckhadden year after year, always hoping to see him.'

'Was he on his own here at the hotel?' asked Agatha.

'Yes.'

'You didn't notice the address on the driving licence?'

She shook her head.

'What about the hotel register?'

'I didn't like to ask.'

Agatha rose to her feet. 'I'll try to find out for you.'

'How?'

'I'm sure they have all the old books locked away somewhere. What year was this?'

'It was in the summer of 1955, in July, around the tenth. But don't tell Jennifer.'

Agatha sat down again. 'Why?'

'I met up with Jennifer ten years afterwards. My parents were poorly and I came here on my own. I told her all about Joseph. She told me I was wasting my life. We became friends.

She had, has, such energy. I was working as a secretary. She told me to take a computer programming course. She said it would get me good money.'

'What did Jennifer do?'

'She was a maths teacher at a London school.'

'Teachers aren't well paid,' Agatha pointed out. 'Why didn't she take a course herself?'

'Jennifer has a vocation for teaching.'

'I see,' commented Agatha drily.

'So I did very well but then my parents died, one after the other, and I had a bit of a breakdown. Jennifer moved in with me in the long summer vac and looked after me. Then she suggested I should sell my parents' house and take a flat with her in London. It seemed such an adventure. I got a programming job with a City firm.'

'But you must have met other people, other men,' said Agatha.

'At first, Jennifer gave a lot of parties but the people that came were mostly schoolteachers. I invited people from the office but they didn't seem to enjoy the parties and they stopped coming.'

'Didn't you make friends with any of the women in the office?'

'Sometimes one of them would suggest we had a drink after work, but Jennifer usually waited for me after work and so . . .'

Jennifer's a leech, thought Agatha.

She stood up again. 'I'll see what I can do with the records.'

Agatha went into Mr Martin's office and asked him if it would be possible to look up old records. He said all the old books were down in the cellars and she was welcome to try but he could not spare any of the staff to help her. He handed Agatha a large key and led her downstairs to the basement and then indicated a low door. 'Down there,' he said. 'You'll find them all stacked on bookshelves at the back of all the junk.'

Agatha unlocked the door and made her way down stone steps. The basement was full of old bits of furniture, dusty curtains, even oil lamps. She picked her way through the clutter to the piles of bound hotel registers, stacked up on shelves in a far corner. To her relief, the date of each was stamped on the outside.

She had to lift down piles of books to get at the one marked '1955'. She sat down on a battered old sofa and opened it, searching until she found July.

She ran her fingers down the entries, glad it was such a small hotel so she did not have a multitude of names to look through. And then she found it, Joseph Brady. Agatha frowned. He had given his address as 92 Sheep Street, Hadderton. What on earth was someone with a car who lived in Hadderton and who could easily have motored over every day doing spending a holiday in an expensive place like the Garden Hotel?

She took a small notebook from her handbag and wrote down the address, put the book back, went upstairs and returned the key to the office and went into the lounge where Mary was still knitting.

'I've found it,' said Agatha.

'You have? Just like that? And after all these years . . .'

'The funny thing is he's given an address in Hadderton, and Hadderton's so close.'

She held out the piece of paper. 'I can't believe it,' whispered Mary.

'We may as well lay your ghost. We'll go tomorrow.'

'It might be a good idea if we didn't tell Jennifer,' said Mary.

'Will that be difficult?'

'I don't think so. I'll say I'm going with you to look at a dress.'

'Right you are. I'll ask the others what they think about the seance when we all meet up tonight.'

Jennifer was scornful of the idea of a seance and said so, loudly. Daisy said she had decided that things like that were best left alone. But the colonel showed unexpected enthusiasm and said it 'sounded like a bit of a lark'. Harry said it would be interesting to see what fraudulent tricks Janine got up to. Daisy capitulated to please the colonel. And so it was decided that Agatha should arrange it for an evening in two days' time. She phoned Janine, who said she would expect them all at nine in the evening.

After dinner, they set out to walk to the dance. They were all unusually silent and Jennifer was openly sulking. She obviously did not like the idea of the seance, but did not want to be left out.

Although they all danced amiably enough that evening, there was an odd sort of constraint which Agatha could not understand. She kept looking towards the doorway of the ballroom, always hoping to see Jimmy arrive, but the evening wore on and there was no sign of him. At last, Daisy said she had a bit of a headache and would like to return to the hotel and the others agreed.

And what was all that about? wondered Agatha as she got ready for bed. Could it be that the idea of the seance frightened one of them and that inner fright had subconsciously communicated itself to the others? Could it be remotely possible that one of them had committed the murder?

And why hadn't Jimmy come? Maybe the love potion wore off after a while.

In the morning, Agatha and a guilty-looking Mary took a cab to Hadderton. 'No trouble getting away?' asked Agatha.

'No, not this time, but she did somehow make me feel guilty.'

'Worse than having a bullying husband.'

'Oh, you mustn't say that, Agatha. Jennifer's the only true friend I've ever had.'

They fell silent as the old cab rattled into Hadderton.

'Sheep Street,' called the taxi driver.

'Ninety-two,' called back Agatha as the cab slowed to a crawl. Sheep Street was lined with red brick houses. Some were smartened up with window-boxes and with the doors and window-sashes painted bright colours. But the others were distinctly seedy. And ninety-two was one of the seedy ones.

'Shouldn't we just leave it alone?' pleaded Mary as Agatha paid off the cab.

'May as well go through with it now we're here.' Agatha marched determinedly up to the front door and knocked on it.

'He probably left here years ago,' said Mary.

The door opened and a very old woman stood there, peering up at them. 'We're looking for Joseph Brady,' said Agatha.

'Come in.' She shuffled off into the interior and they followed her. The living-room into which she led them was dark and furnished with battered old chairs and a sagging sofa.

'This is Mary Dulsey and I am Agatha Raisin,' began Agatha. 'Mary knew Joseph when he was much younger. She always wondered what became of him. Do you know him?'

'He's my son.'

They both looked at the old woman. She eased herself into an armchair. Her hands were knobbly with arthritis and her face was seamed and wrinkled.

Mary seemed to have been struck dumb. 'Where is he?' asked Agatha.

Mrs Brady gave a wheezy little sigh. 'Doing time.'

'Why, what for?' asked Agatha, ignoring Mary's yelp of distress.

'Same old business. Stealing cars.' She peered at Mary. 'How did you know him?'

Mary found her voice, albeit a trembling voice. 'It was years ago, in 1955. At Wyckhadden. At the Garden Hotel.'

Mrs Brady nodded. 'That would be about the first time he got into trouble.'

'With the police?' asked Agatha.

'Yes,' she said wearily. 'He was working as a car salesman for a firm in Hadderton. He'd just got his driving licence. He stole a car and he stole the money from the firm's office. He said afterwards that he had planned to go to a posh hotel and look for a rich girl.' The old eyes looked sympathetically at Mary. 'Was that you, dear?'

'I suppose so,' said Mary miserably. 'We weren't rich. My father was only a lawyer.'

'That would be rich to Joseph. We never had much, see. Well, the police got him a couple of days after he came back. How he thought he'd get away with it, I don't know. He'd left the stolen car in a side street, as if someone else had pinched it. But he'd left his fingerprints all over the office at the car firm and the police found the rest of the money hidden in his room. He swore he'd never do anything like that again. He got a light sentence, but it was hard to get work with a criminal record. He left home one day shortly after that. Said he was going to Australia. Then, four years later, he wrote to me from prison. Cars again and a longer sentence. Then it was burglary. The latest was stealing cars and driving them over to some crooked dealer in Bulgaria.'

'Have you a recent photograph?' asked Agatha.

Mrs Brady rose painfully from her chair and lifted a cardboard box down from a shelf beside the fireplace. She rested it on a small table, and putting on a pair of spectacles, began to look through the photographs. She lifted one out and handed it to Mary. 'That you, miss?'

Mary looked down at a picture of herself and Joseph on the prom at Wyckhadden. 'Yes,' she said in a choked voice. 'One of those beach photographers took that picture. One for me, one for Joseph.'

'Here's one taken before his last sentence.' Mrs Brady handed Mary a photograph. Agatha joined Mary and looked down at it. The Joseph in this picture was baring a set of false teeth at the camera. He was nearly bald and his weaselly face bore little resemblance to the young man on the prom.

Agatha looked at Mary's shocked face. 'Thank you for your time, Mrs Brady. We are really sorry to have troubled you.'

'I'll see you to the door,' she said. 'Funny, there was always some girl or another over the years that he'd said he was going to marry, but the law always caught up with him first.'

Out in the street, Mary walked a little way with Agatha and then broke down and cried and cried, saying over and over again in between sobs, 'How could you have done this to me, Agatha?'

'But you wanted to find him,' protested Agatha, but feeling guilty all the same. It would have been better to have left poor Mary with her dream intact. A cold wind whistled down Sheep Street. Wind chimes hung over a door tinkled their foreign exotic sound.

'Let's find a pub,' said Agatha.

They turned the corner of Sheep Street and found a small pub. Agatha ordered brandies. Mary drank and sobbed and sobbed and drank. Agatha waited patiently. At last Mary dried her eyes and blew her nose.

'All these years,' she said, 'I've carried this bright dream of Joseph. One day he would come back if only I kept going to Wyckhadden. I put up with Jennifer because I had this dream. Now I have nothing.'

'I wish I had left things alone,' said Agatha. 'But how were we to know he'd turn out to be a criminal?'

'It's not really your fault. I had to know,' said Mary. 'I'll have to tell Jennifer.'

'Why?'

'She'll know something is up with me.'

'Oh, well, tell her if you must,' said Agatha, suddenly weary of the whole business. There was a cigarette machine in the corner of the pub. She looked at it longingly. But it was years and years since she had gone so long without a cigarette. Stick it out, Agatha!

Back at the hotel, Agatha found Jimmy waiting for her. He looked curiously at red-eyed Mary, who darted past him and up the stairs. 'What's up with her?'

'Let's go for a walk and I'll tell you about it.'

Once out on the promenade, he took Agatha's arm and said, 'You smell of brandy. Starting early?'

'Consoling Mary.' As they walked along, Agatha told him about Joseph.

'Poor woman,' he said when Agatha had finished. 'I could have found all that out for her.'

'I never thought of asking you. Mary didn't think for a minute that he was a criminal.'

Agatha then told him about the seance. 'We've still got our eye on Janine's husband. You should be careful.'

'I thought he had a cast-iron alibi.'

'I'm always suspicious of people with cast-iron alibis.'

'Why did you call to see me, Jimmy?'

'I wanted to ask you out for dinner tonight. There's this new Italian restaurant.'

'I would love to.'

'That's fine. I'll pick you up at eight. I'd better walk you back now. I've a lot of paperwork to do.'

Tired after all the morning's emotion, Agatha planned to lie down that afternoon and then enjoy a leisurely time getting ready for her date. She was just about to pull her sweater over her head when there came a peremptory knocking at the door. She tugged down her sweater and went to open it. Jennifer stood there, her fists clenched and eyes blazing with anger. 'I want a word with you, you interfering bitch!'

'Come in,' said Agatha wearily.

Jennifer strode into the room. 'You have destroyed Mary's happiness. She needed that dream.'

Agatha looked at her in sudden dislike. 'You destroyed Mary's dreams,' she said furiously. 'You've hung on to her like a leech for years. What chance did she ever have to make other friends with you around?'

'How dare you? Who nursed her back to

health after her parents' death? Who steered her into a profitable occupation?'

'You did. So much easier than doing anything about your own life. You're not angry, Jennifer. You're frightened. As long as Mary had the dream of Joseph coming back, you were safe. Without her dream, she's going to look back on a wasted life.'

Jennifer turned an ugly muddy colour. 'Just keep out of her life or it'll be the worse for you.'

She strode out and slammed the door. Agatha sat down, her legs shaking. Now there was surely someone who could have committed murder. She tried to have a nap that afternoon but could not sleep. She was torn between leaving Wyckhadden and escaping from what looked like an ugly situation with Jennifer and staying and finding out more about the murder. And then there was Jimmy. After Charles's fickle unfaithfulness and James Lacey's coldness, it was wonderful to have some man really keen on her. Perhaps they could get married.

Agatha phoned Mrs Bloxby at the vicarage in Carsely. 'How nice to hear from you,' cried Mrs Bloxby. 'We're all wondering when you're coming back. Not getting too much involved in this nasty murder?'

Agatha settled down to tell her all about the murder, the residents at the hotel, her growing friendship with Jimmy, and the row with Jennifer.

'I wouldn't blame Jennifer too much,' said Mrs Bloxby when Agatha had finished. 'I have met many women like Mary. If it hadn't been Jennifer, it would have been someone very like her. Or it could have been a bullying man. You will probably find that her parents were rather domineering. And this Jimmy of yours sounds hopeful.'

'How's James?' asked Agatha abruptly.

'He seems very well.' Mrs Bloxby was not going to tell Agatha that James had been asking about her. Let Agatha progress with Jimmy.

'And my cats?'

'Doris Simpson is looking after them very well. We're all missing you.'

'Just a few more days and then I'll probably be home.'

When Agatha rang off, she suddenly remembered Janine's grim remark that she would never have sex again. 'We'll see about that,' thought Agatha as she shaved her legs, and then rubbed Lancôme's Poème body lotion into her skin.

The evening began as a success. Jimmy told stories about his job in Wyckhadden and Agatha replied with tales of Carsely and the residents, although she did not mention James.

He drove her back to the hotel and then turned and gathered her in his arms. 'Oh, Agatha,' he said huskily and kissed her. Agatha replied with a passion that surprised her. Damn that witch. She would prove her wrong. 'Can't we go to your place for a night-cap?' she whispered.

'Right,' he said in a choked voice. He drove up to the back part of the town and parked outside a trim bungalow. Like two people squaring up for a fight, they walked up the path side by side, the tension rising between them. It shouldn't be like this, thought Agatha. We should still be laughing and giggling.

He led her into the bungalow, neat, sparse and brightly lit. 'The bathroom's there,' he said. 'I'll use the other one.'

'Two bathrooms,' said Agatha, striving for a light note. 'How posh.'

'I took in lodgers at one time. Now I can't be bothered.'

Agatha went into the sparkling-clean bathroom with its Nile-green bath and loo. She undressed and ran a bath. She wished she had a night-gown or dressing-gown. She finally emerged from the bathroom wearing nothing more than a black lacy slip.

'Where are you?' she called.

'Here!'

She followed the sound of his voice and found herself in a bedroom. Jimmy was lying in a double bed, the duvet up to his chin, his face grim. Oh, well, here goes, thought Agatha. At least I'm about to prove Janine wrong.

She climbed into the bed beside him. The sheets were slippery and cold and his body was cold. She began to kiss him.

At last he turned away from her. 'I'm sorry, Agatha. I can't. Not yet. I thought I could but I can't.'

'I'll go, then,' said Agatha in a small voice. He did not reply. She climbed out of bed and looked back from the doorway. He was scrunched up on his side, his eyes tight closed.

Agatha found her way back to the bathroom. She put on her clothes and went into the hall, where she had seen a phone and phone books. She looked up taxis in the Yellow Pages and phoned for a cab. They asked for the address. Fortunately for Agatha, it was stamped on one of the phone books because she did not have the slightest idea where she was.

As she waited for the cab, she wondered whether she should go in and console Jimmy. But she felt rejected, felt a failure. What a rotten day.

She heaved a sigh of relief when she heard the cab pulling up. As it cruised through the silent night-time streets of Wyckhadden, she felt small and grubby and unwanted. Stay for the seance and then go home, home to Carsely.

Agatha went down for breakfast the following morning. They all, with the exception of

Jennifer and Mary, greeted her amiably enough. Mary's eyes looked puffy with weeping.

I'm too upset about myself to worry about her, thought Agatha, angry with herself for still feeling guilty about Mary. I'm the dream murderer, she said to herself. First Mary then Jimmy, and all in one day. Damn that Janine. That's what made me rush Jimmy.

She ate a light breakfast of poached eggs on toast. Again, as she sipped her coffee, she thought longingly of how good a cigarette would taste. There was no cigarette machine in the hotel – nothing so vulgar. But there was one on the pier which had, remarkably enough in these wicked days, not been vandalized.

A good walk would take her mind off things. She walked miles that day along the beach by the restless sea. Then she returned to the hotel to tell the manager that she would be checking out on Saturday, in two days' time, and to get her bill ready. The sudden relief that she had made a definite decision to go home brightened her up.

As she was getting ready to go out for the seance that evening, there was a knock at the door. Agatha looked round the room for something to use as a weapon, decided she was paranoid, and opened the door and backed away from it quickly when she saw Jennifer standing there.

'I came to apologize,' said Jennifer gruffly. 'You only did it to help Mary. She had to know.'

'That's all right, then,' said Agatha, relieved. 'Looking forward to the seance this evening?'

'Not particularly. Though I wouldn't mind exposing her as a fraud.'

'But I thought you believed in her mother's medicines!'

'There's a lot to be said for old country remedies. But when it comes to fortune-telling and seances, I've never believed in that tommy-rot.'

'Neither do I,' said Agatha, who had no intention of telling Jennifer she'd had her palm read. 'But that's why I think it will be quite fun – I mean, to see what tricks she gets up to. Daisy believes in seances, I gather.'

'She did for a bit, but then she decided that Francie was a charlatan.'

'How did she come to that conclusion? I wonder. It was she who sent me to Francie in the first place.'

'Oh, I think she believed in her potions. I'd better go and get ready. What are you wearing?'

'I don't feel like dressing up tonight,' said Agatha. 'The weather's turned awfully cold. I wish I still had my fur coat.'

'A lot of people don't approve of the wearing of fur,' said Jennifer. 'It could happen again if you got another.'

'You're right,' said Agatha ruefully. 'They'll soon be stoning us in restaurants for eating meat, and all the animals will be killed off and we'll be left with only token species in zoos.'

'Samuel Butler said if you carried that sort of argument to its logical conclusion, we'll all end up eating cabbages which have been humanely put to death.'

'Who's Samuel Butler? Someone in this nanny government we've got?'

'He was a Victorian philosopher.'

'Oh,' said Agatha uncomfortably. She hated having the vast gaps in her literary education exposed.

'I'll leave you to it.' Jennifer held out her hand. 'No hard feelings?'

'None at all.' Agatha felt her hand seized in a crushing grip like a man's.

After Jennifer had left, and Agatha had just finished dressing, her phone rang. She ran to answer it. 'Jimmy?' she said.

'No, it's Harry here,' creaked the elderly voice. 'We're all ready to leave. The colonel's booked two taxis. Too cold to walk.'

'Be right down,' said Agatha. She replaced the receiver. Jimmy might at least have called.

They set out in their taxis. Agatha wondered what had happened between Mary and Jennifer to heal the breach. Mary was looking quite cheerful and once more she and Jennifer seemed the best of friends. Well, thought Agatha, I suppose Mary's too old to change the habit of a lifetime.

Janine's husband ushered them in. They crowded in the small hall removing coats and hats. Then he guided them through to a back room. It was brightly lit and furnished only with a round table covered in a black velvet cloth.

They seated themselves round it. 'This is jolly exciting,' said the colonel. 'If it looks like ectoplasm, it's probably our Agatha having a sneaky cigarette.' They all laughed except Agatha who said, 'I haven't had a cigarette in ages. I'm cured.'

The room became filled with strange sounds. 'What on earth is that?' asked Harry.

'Whales,' said Daisy. 'It's a tape of the noises whales make. You can buy one in these Mystique shops.'

Mary gave a nervous laugh. 'I never knew any whales.'

'I saw some performing dolphins in Florida once,' said the colonel. 'Jolly clever beasts. Do you know . . .'

He broke off because Janine had entered the room. She was dressed in a long white muslin gown, very plain, with long tight sleeves and a high neck. Agatha eyed her curiously. How could she hold this seance, agree to this seance, with her mother so recently dead? And yet, thought Agatha, peering at her closely, despite her heavy make-up, her eyes had the red, strained look of someone who had done a lot of weeping recently.

'Shall we begin?' she said, sitting down. 'Please hold hands and keep holding hands. The circle must not be broken.' The overhead lights were turned off. Now there was only a bluish light shining down on Janine and spotlights that lit up their joined hands around the table, but leaving their faces in darkness.

Agatha was between Daisy and the colonel.

There was a long silence. The whale sounds died away. Janine sat with her head back.

Then she closed her eyes and said in a crooning monotone. 'Who is there?'

And then a man's voice said, 'Hello, Aggie?'

Agatha tensed.

'It's me, your husband Jimmy Raisin.'

Agatha's skin crawled. Jimmy's accent had been a mixture of Cockney and Irish, just like this voice. Her mind raced. Of course his murder had been in all the papers and his background.

'I'm waiting for you, Aggie,' he said. 'It won't be long now.'

'Can I ask him something?' said Agatha.

Janine sat with her eyes closed. So Agatha said, 'Do you remember our holiday here in Wyckhadden, Jimmy? That's why I came back.'

'And that's how I knew where to find you,' said the cocky voice cheerfully.

Agatha relaxed. She and Jimmy had never been in Wyckhadden.

'That's funny,' she said. 'Because we were never . . .'

'Someone else wants to get in,' intoned Janine.

There was a long silence. A gust of wind suddenly howled down the lane outside. Appropriate atmospherics, thought Agatha cynically, and yet she was aware of the tension building in the room, of the colonel holding her hand so tightly that she could feel her wedding ring digging into her finger. Silly and old-fashioned to keep wearing a wedding ring, she thought inconsequentially. She cleared her throat. Nothing was happening. The woman was a charlatan. It was time to leave.

And then a low moan escaped Janine's lips and she began to rock backwards and forwards. A thin line of grey smoke escaped from between her lips and hung in the bluish light above her head. Can't be cigarette smoke, thought Agatha. Wonder how she does that? But there was something eerie and unearthly in the moaning. Janine's eyes were tightly closed. Then a thin voice sounded from Janine's lips.

'Hello, daughter. I have now completed my journey to the other side.'

'Mother. How are you?'

'Restless,' wailed the voice. 'My death is not yet avenged.'

'It will be, mother. Who killed you?'

'I know who killed me.'

There was a tense silence and then Mary screamed and leapt to her feet. 'What is it?' asked the colonel. 'What's up, my dear? Dammit, I've had enough of this nonsense.' He walked over to the door and switched on the light.

'Someone kicked me hard,' said Mary.

'You have broken the circle and broken the spell,' said Janine furiously. 'I cannot do anything more.'

'You can't expect us to fork out two hundred pounds for this charade,' said the colonel.

Janine's husband came into the room. 'What's going on?'

'These people broke the circle just when I had got in touch with mother and now they're refusing to pay.' Janine suddenly buried her head in her hands and began to cry.

Cliff suddenly looked menacing. 'We'll see about that.'

'Yes we will see about that,' said the colonel wrathfully. 'Either we all leave peacefully or I will call the police to escort us out of here.'

'Let them go,' said Janine, drying her eyes. 'Let the bastards go.' They made for the door. 'I put a curse on you all,' said Janine.

Daisy gave a terrified little squeak and pressed against the colonel.

* * *

'We may as well walk,' said the colonel when they were all gathered outside. 'What did you think of all that, Agatha? Did that sound like your husband?'

'It did a bit,' said Agatha, 'but he was murdered and the murder background was in all the papers. Besides, I'd never been in Wyckhadden before and neither had he.'

Daisy shivered as they walked along the prom which was glittering with frost. 'She cursed us.'

'She only cursed us because she didn't get any money,' said the colonel soothingly. 'I think what we all need is a drink and a quiet game of Scrabble.'

While they played Scrabble, Agatha began to wonder about that supposed conjuring up of Francie's spirit. Surely it meant that Janine suspected one of them. And had someone really kicked Mary? Or had Mary been frightened that she was about to be exposed? But Mary was a dainty little thing. Agatha could not imagine her striking such a blow as to kill Francie. And yet a desperate woman *could* have struck that blow. But why was Francie's door unlocked? Had the murderer a key and then gone away, leaving the door unlocked? Jimmy had said nothing about the body having been moved. Therefore whoever had killed her, had killed her in her bedroom.

So her thoughts raced on and she got chided by the others for playing badly. None of this elderly lot could be guilty, thought Agatha. Just look how they all concentrated on the game.

At last they all went up to their respective rooms and were enclosed in the hotel's usual expensive night-time hush. When Agatha passed the reception desk on her way up, she noticed the night porter was asleep on a chair behind the desk. Anyone could come or go without his noticing, thought Agatha bitterly. He had probably been asleep when that wretched girl walked in and sabotaged my coat.

The morning dawned, clear and frosty with a pale sun shining down on a calm sea.

After breakfast the colonel, who seemed in good spirits, suggested they all take a stroll along the pier. 'I want to show you a bit where the pier is becoming definitely unsafe,' he said. 'These old Victorian piers are part of Britain's heritage. Perhaps, if you all agree with me, we could get up a petition.'

Well wrapped up, hatted and gloved and wearing warm coats, they all walked along the pier – like some geriatric school outing, thought Agatha.

The colonel stopped them half-way along. 'Now I want you all to lean over and look down at the piles. They are covered in layers of seaweed but definitely rotted in some parts. The sea is very calm today, so you should all be able to get a good look at what I'm talking about.'

They dutifully leaned over. Glassy rolling waves surged under the pier.

'What's that white thing in the water?' asked Jennifer.

'Where?' asked Mary.

'Just there.' Jennifer pointed. Then she said huskily, 'Oh, my God.'

The white thing rolled over on a wave and the dead face of Janine stared up at them, her blonde hair floating out about her head, her muslin dress floating about her body.

Chapter Five

Mary was sobbing into Jennifer's flat chest. She's not wearing that padded bra I recommended, thought Agatha numbly. Daisy was trembling and weeping. Harry Berry was sitting on the boards on the pier, his old head in his hands. And the tall figure of the colonel could be seen striding off down the pier to call the police.

Agatha fumbled in her handbag for her change purse. She extracted three pound coins and a fifty-pence piece and walked to the cigarette machine. She put in the coins and pressed a button. A cigarette packet rattled down into the tray below. Agatha picked it up, stripped off the wrapping, extracted a cigarette and put it in her mouth. She lit it up and took a deep draw. Her head swam and she felt dizzy. She staggered to the rail and hung on, but she took another puff. A sea-gull alighted on the rail next to her and gazed at her assessingly with its beady prehistoric eyes.

Some teenagers came down the pier, laughing and chattering. One of them spied the figure of Harry and stopped. 'What's up, guv?' he called. 'Want us to call a doctor?'

Harry shook his head. 'There's a body in the water,' he said hoarsely.

'Cor!' The teenagers ran to the rail.

If it wasn't that husband of hers, it was one of us, thought Agatha. Surely we were the last to see her.

The wail of police sirens tore through the air. Blue lights flashed at the end of the pier. The tall figure of the colonel came into view. Beside him walked Detective Constable Ian Tarret and Detective Sergeant Peter Carroll. Behind them came more police.

'Stand back!' ordered Tarret. 'Who spotted the body?'

Agatha found her voice. 'We did. Us from the hotel.'

His eyes bored into her. 'You again. Move along,' he said to the teenagers. 'The rest of you stay where you are.'

Agatha began to shiver. Then she saw Jimmy hurrying along the pier, his long black coat flapping. Tarret led him to the rail and pointed down.

'If I may make a suggestion?' said the colonel.

'Yes?' Jimmy looked at him, his eyes first sliding past Agatha. 'As none of us had anything to do with this outrage, I suggest as we are all elderly and the day is cold, we should be allowed to return to the hotel where we will await your questions.'

Agatha, despite her shock, did not like being included in that 'elderly'.

'Very well,' said Jimmy. He called forward a policeman. 'Go with them and keep a watch on them until I can get to them.'

They helped Harry to his feet. Then they followed the policeman down the pier past gawping onlookers and so to the hotel. Mr Martin, the manager, came to meet them. 'What now?' he cried. In a few succinct sentences, the colonel told him. 'We will all foregather in the lounge,' he said. 'Is the fire made up?'

'Not yet.' Mr Martin rubbed his hands in distress. 'This is terrible, terrible.'

'Get someone to light the fire,' barked the colonel.

They trooped into the lounge and collapsed into chairs around the fire. 'I think tea with a lot of sugar,' said the colonel, pressing the bell on the wall.

Agatha lit another cigarette. I quit once. I can quit again, she told herself with the true optimism of the addict.

Mary had stopped crying but she was very white. Daisy kept letting out odd little whimpers of distress and looking to the colonel for sympathy. But the colonel was watching the hotel servant lighting the fire, his head sunk on his chest.

Through the long window, Agatha could see Janine's husband hurrying along the pier. He would tell the police about the seance. She turned to the others. 'I wonder if it was the husband after all.'

No one replied. Tea arrived and the colonel poured. They all helped themselves to milk and sugar and digestive biscuits.

'I wonder what happened? I wonder who did it?' Agatha asked desperately.

'Put lots of sugar in your tea, Daisy,' urged the colonel.

Agatha looked at them in bewilderment. All of them were avoiding eye contact with her. Were they *all* in it?

Jimmy Jessop came into the lounge. 'The manager has kindly let us use the office, which will save all of you going down to the police station. I will take you one at a time. You first, Mrs Raisin. You will all have to come to the police station later on today to make official statements.'

Agatha followed him into the office, where Detective Sergeant Peter Carroll was waiting. Jimmy looked at her as if he had never seen her before. 'The dead woman's husband said you were all at a seance last night. Begin there and tell us what happened.'

So Agatha began. She described the seance. She described how she had heard the supposed voice of her dead husband. 'I always thought the voice of the dead was supposed to come from the medium's mouth,' she said, 'but this voice was in the room.'

'And what did this voice say?'

'Just a lot of rot,' said Agatha. 'How was I, things like that.'

'And then?'

'And then the supposed voice of Francie filled the room. She got to the point when she told Janine she knew who had murdered her and then Mary screamed. She said someone had kicked her. The colonel said we weren't paying, Cliff got ugly, the colonel threatened to call the police and so we all got out of there. We went for a walk on the pier this morning and Jennifer spotted the body in the water, or rather she said something like, "What's that white thing?" and when we looked over, the body turned in the water and we saw it was Janine. The body was below the surface but the water was clear and glassy so we all saw it was her.'

'Nothing else you can think of?'

'Like what?'

'Like what were the reactions of the others when you all saw the body?'

'Harry Berry slumped down and sat on the pier as if his legs had given way. Mary was holding on to Jennifer and crying. Daisy was squeaking and whimpering. The colonel went off to call the police.'

'And you?'

'I went and bought a packet of cigarettes from the machine on the pier. I'd given up smoking, but suddenly, more than anything, I wanted a cigarette.'

'That will be all for now. Send the colonel in.'

Agatha rose. 'Jimmy, could I have a word with you in private?'

Carroll glared.

'No, you can't,' said Jimmy coldly. 'Send the colonel in.'

All Agatha had wanted to do was to apologize to him for rushing him. Feeling very low, she told the colonel to go in and sat by the fire. She lit another cigarette and stared moodily at the others. It was odd. Surely it was odd that this second murder, this murder of a woman they had all seen last night, should not be discussed amongst them. She got up and went to the window. A boat was bobbing by the pier. She watched, fascinated, as the body of Janine was lifted aboard. A team of divers arrived. Why? They had the body. Evidence, of course. They would be searching on the sea-bed for some sort of weapon. How did she die? And if someone had thrown her from the pier, where was her coat? It had been bitterly cold last night. Janine would not have gone out wearing nothing but a thin muslin gown. Cliff could have killed her, thrown the body in the sea, and the currents could have carried it round to the pier.

Surely Cliff was the murderer. He stood to

gain not only Janine's money but the money she had inherited from her mother, and she must have inherited Francie's house and money or she would not have moved into that house in Partons Lane.

If only the police would decide it was Cliff. If they did not arrest him, then she would be trapped in Wyckhadden. She thought of her cottage, of her cats, Hodge and Boswell, of James Lacey, of her neighbours, and she began to tremble and her eyes filled with tears.

'Going up to my room,' she said gruffly.

No one replied.

Agatha went upstairs. She collapsed on the bed and in a minute she was fast asleep.

She was awakened two hours later by a knocking at the door. She struggled up off the bed and went to answer it. A policewoman stood there. 'You are to accompany me to the station.'

'Wait a minute,' said Agatha, thinking of Jimmy. 'I'd better put some make-up on.'

She went into the bathroom and quickly cleaned her face and put on fresh make-up. Then she remembered that love potion. Francie had said five drops. Five drops would leave enough to analyse when she got home. She slipped the bottle into her handbag and went out to join the policewoman.

Back again to the station, back to the interview room. Agatha sat down on a hard chair.

The policewoman came in with a tray with a teapot, milk and sugar and a china mug, and a paper cup of coffee. She handed Agatha the paper cup. 'Who's the tea for?' asked Agatha, looking at the coffee with distaste. 'That's for the inspector,' was the reply.

'Lucy!' called a voice from outside in the corridor. Lucy put the tray down on the table and went out. Agatha could hear her speaking to someone outside. Quick as a flash, Agatha whipped out the bottle of love potion and, with one eye on the door, tipped a little into the teapot.

The policewoman came back in and picked up the tray and departed. Agatha sat alone. She was just about to rise and shout down the corridor for someone when the door opened and Tarret and Carroll came in, accompanied by a policewoman. Tarret and Carroll sat opposite Agatha, the policewoman switched on the recording machine, and the interview began.

This time the questions were more searching. The police had learned from the others that the seance had been Agatha's idea. Why?

'It seemed a bit of a lark,' said Agatha weakly.

'A lark that led to murder. Now let's go over everything from the beginning.'

After an hour of close questioning, Agatha began to wonder if people confessed to the murder of someone, a murder they had not committed, out of sheer weariness and a sense of unnatural guilt caused by the beady, suspicious eyes of detectives.

At last she was free to go but told not to leave Wyckhadden.

As she was leaving the police station, she was called back by the desk sergeant. 'The inspector wants a word with you.' He buzzed her through the door beside the desk and then led her along a corridor to a room at the end, opened the door, and said, 'Mrs Raisin, sir.'

Jimmy rose to meet her. Agatha's eyes flew to the tea-tray, which was balanced on the top of book shelves. Had he drunk any?

'Sit down, Agatha,' said Jimmy. 'I've got a minute or two free.'

'I'm sorry about the other night,' said Agatha. She decided to tell him the truth. 'I went to see Janine to see if I could get more of that hair tonic of her mother's. She didn't have any but she offered to read my palm. She said I would have no more adventures. She also said I would never have sex again. I wanted to prove her wrong. You mustn't worry about it. It doesn't mean there's anything wrong with you. It happens to lots of men.'

Jimmy looked at her intently. 'You're not just saying that to comfort me? About it happening to a lot of men?'

'No, it really does. I thought you would know that.'

He smiled. 'It's hardly the thing men talk about and in this station, you would think we were all a virile lot, to hear the stories in the canteen. The fact is, my wife was my first and my last.'

'There you are!' said Agatha. 'It stands to reason. If it weren't for this wretched murder, we could take it slowly, become friends first.'

'We could still manage that. I'm afraid you're trapped here for a bit longer.'

'How did she die?'

'She drowned, or so the preliminary examination suggests. Her husband said she couldn't swim.'

'Has he been arrested?'

'No, he's been taken in for questioning, but I don't think we can hold him.'

'Why?'

'Some elderly lady in one of those boarding-houses on the front is awake for a good part of the night. She said it was around two in the morning. She saw Janine hurrying along the prom in the direction of the pier.'

'Surely not in that white dress. It was freezing cold.'

'The witness said Janine had a big black cloak on, and they recovered a cloak from the sea. Then she said she saw Cliff. He ran a little way after her. She turned round and shouted, "Go back to the house. Leave me alone. I know what I'm doing." She said Cliff turned back. She sat at the window, reading and occasionally looking out. She said she sat there until dawn and never saw either of them again.'

'But,' exclaimed Agatha, 'if Janine said she knew what she was doing, somehow that suggests that Cliff knew who she was going to meet.'

'That's what we thought,' said Jimmy. 'But so far Cliff is sticking to his story, which is that Janine had received a phone call. She got up and got dressed. He said he was sleepy and it was only when he heard the street door slam behind her that he thought it was odd.

'He ran after her but she told him to go home. He says he doesn't know who phoned or who she was meeting.'

'But that phone call could be traced.'

'It was made from a phone-box at the entrance to the pier, so we're none the wiser. We're under a lot of pressure. The newspaper headlines will be screaming about the witch murders tomorrow and already the town's filling up with photographers and reporters and television crews with their satellite dishes. I've got the chief constable on my back. The superintendent from Hadderton is coming down to take over. I'm relieved in a way. It takes some of the pressure off me.'

'You know what I find odd?' said Agatha. 'That lot at the hotel. First there's the seance, which Mary broke up as soon as the supposed spirit of Francie was about to accuse someone. Then they don't talk about the murders, none of them do. This evening the colonel will probably suggest a game of Scrabble. They will make little jokes about the meaning of words, Harry Berry will add up the scores, I will be bottom of the league as usual, and that will be that.'

'The colonel did say that the whole business was distasteful and best forgotten about. It's maybe the way his generation goes on.'

'Rubbish,' said Agatha roundly. 'No one can ignore two murders.'

'Thanks for coming to see me, Agatha. I'd better get to work again, but I'll call on you as soon as I get some free time.'

Agatha gathered up her handbag and gloves. She took a quick glance at the tea-tray. The cup had been used.

He opened the door for her and bent down and kissed her cheek. 'You won't be bothered with press at the hotel. Mr Martin is not allowing any of them to stay.'

When Agatha went into the dining-room that night, she found their numbers had been augmented by a man and woman. She studied them closely. They were sharing a bottle of claret and talking in low voices. The woman had short-cropped dark hair and was wearing a pin-striped trouser suit. The man was in a respectable charcoal-grey suit and modest tie. But there was a certain air of raffishness about him, and when Agatha entered the dining-room his eyes raked her up and down and he whispered something to the woman, who looked at Agatha as well.

Agatha sighed and turned about and went to the manager's office. 'I thought you weren't going to let the press into the hotel,' she said.

'I haven't,' said Mr Martin. 'I've been very strict about that. The life-blood of this little hotel is supplied by the residents.'

'You've got two of them in the dining-room right now. Man and a woman.'

'But that is a Mr and Mrs Devenish, over here from Devon.'

'Did you ask for any identification?'

'No, we don't, if people are British. They sign the registration form and the visitors' book.'

Mr Martin surveyed her with disfavour. 'I have been manager of this hotel for fifteen years, Mrs Raisin, and I pride myself on being a good judge of character.'

'And I pride myself on being a good judge of the press. Come with me,' said Agatha wearily.

'If you make a scene, I will never forgive you.' But Mr Martin followed her from the office. Agatha went straight up to the table where the couple were sitting. 'Which newspaper do you represent?' she asked.

The man and woman exchanged quick glances. 'We're just here on holiday,' the man said.

'Then you will not mind if Mr Martin here asks you for some sort of identification. I am sure you would not like me to call the police in to check your credentials.'

'Okay, then,' said the woman with a shrug. 'We're from the *Daily Bugle*. So what's wrong with that?'

'I'll leave you to deal with it,' said Agatha to the outraged manager and went back to her table.

As she watched the press being told to leave, Agatha began to think again about the hotel residents. Just supposing one of them was a murderer. Did ordinary people such as they suddenly become murderous, or was there something in their backgrounds which would give her a clue? How could she find out? The police would simply check their records and if none of them had a record, they would not probe any further. Mary had suffered a nervous breakdown. But so did lots of people. She had learned a lot about Mary because of her love for Joseph Brady. The best way to get the others to talk was to get them alone. She decided to start with the colonel.

The colonel finished his dinner first and went through to the lounge. Agatha knew he would soon be followed by the rest and then that wretched Scrabble board would be brought out. She followed him into the lounge.

'Colonel,' said Agatha, 'I wonder if I could ask you a favour?'

'Certainly.'

'I am upset and uneasy. This second murder has really frightened me. I wondered if I could persuade you to come for a walk with me and perhaps stop somewhere for a drink? I know it's silly of me, but I feel I have to get out of the hotel and I am frightened to go on my own.'

He rose gallantly to his feet. 'I'll tell the others.'

'Do you mind if we don't? I don't feel like a crowd. You are such a sensible gentleman. I feel if I could talk to you about things, I would not feel so frightened.'

'Of course. Shall we get our coats? It's cold out.'

When they emerged from the hotel, they blinked in the glare of television lights and flashlights. 'We have nothing to say,' said the colonel firmly, taking Agatha's arm and shouldering his way through the pack. 'No, really. This is harassment.'

Agatha prayed that some more enterprising reporter would not break away from the pack and follow them. But the press too often hunted together, which is why a lot of them often missed out on stories, and they were left in peace.

A thin veil of cloud was covering the moon and the air felt damp. 'Rain coming,' said the colonel.

'The weather has been very changeable,' said Agatha, thinking two brutal murders have been committed and here we are, talking about the weather.

'I've been thinking,' began the colonel.

'Yes?' said Agatha eagerly.

'That last Scrabble game, Harry put down "damn". Now I pointed out we weren't allowed any swear words and if you remember he became quite angry, so I let it go.'

'It's a verb,' said Agatha crossly, 'as in damn with faint praise.'

The colonel's face cleared. 'How clever of you. I shall apologize to Harry.'

It was James Lacey who had quoted that once, thought Agatha bleakly.

'I think we should go to the Metropol for a drink,' said the colonel. 'It's rather a flashy sort of modern place, but the cocktail bar is suitable for ladies.'

The Metropol catered for the smarter, flashier, more painted geriatric. Women's faces were grouted with layers of foundation cream. Face-lifts were still rare in England.

'I like trying new cocktails,' said the colonel, studying a card on the small plastic table. 'There's one here, the Wyckhadden Slammer. Let's try two of those.' He signalled to the cocktail waitress, a large elderly woman with a truculent face, and ordered the drinks. When they arrived, they turned out to be bright blue in colour with a great deal of fruit and with little umbrellas sticking out of the top.

'I wanted to talk about the murders,' began Agatha.

'Now why does a pretty lady like you want to talk about nasty things like that?' said the colonel roguishly. 'This is quite good.' He sipped his cocktail. 'Wonder how they get that blue colour?'

'I keep wondering who did it?'

'Oh, I'd leave that to the police. They may seem to be plodding but they are very thorough. They'll get there.'

'Have you no curiosity about the murders?'

The colonel took another sip of his blue drink. 'Not really. You see, I'm pretty sure it was the husband.'

Agatha decided to try another tack. 'Have you and the other residents known each other long?'

'Years, I suppose. We all used to come here on holiday and then, as we retired, we decided to stay.'

'It's an expensive hotel.'

'Mr Martin is only too keen to give us special rates. Can't get people in the winter. Then there's all those silly people who go abroad for their holidays now. Why?'

'Sunshine?'

'Pah, all that does is cause skin cancer. The British skin was never meant to be exposed to the sun.'

'Did your wife come here with you?'

'Gudren enjoyed it here, yes. When I was in military service we travelled a lot, but we always tried to get here when I was on leave.'

'Don't any of you stay with your families?'

'I have a son. I stay with him at Christmas. Daisy goes to her sister then, Harry to his daughter, and – let me see – I think Jennifer and Mary stay on.'

'Do you ever quarrel? I mean, spending so much time together, year in and year out.'

'Quarrel? I don't think we have anything to quarrel about.' The colonel looked genuinely puzzled.

Agatha gave a little sigh. She was not going to get anything else out of the colonel. She would need to try one of the others. She refused his offer of another drink and said she was feeling tired. They walked back to the hotel.

'Press have given up for the night,' said the colonel cheerfully.

'Let's hope some big story breaks and takes them somewhere else,' said Agatha. 'Oh, there's Jimmy.' The tall figure of the inspector could be seen standing on the hotel steps.

'I'll leave you to it,' said the colonel.

'Agatha,' said Jimmy with a shy smile. 'I was hoping to have a word with you. The others are playing Scrabble in the lounge. Let's go to our pub.'

Our pub, thought Agatha cheerfully. I can't wait to try that love potion on James Lacey.

'Now, what's happening?' asked Agatha when they were seated over drinks.

Jimmy sighed. 'We're going to have to release the husband. We haven't anything on him.'

'Don't you have anything at all? What about all the wonders of forensic science? Isn't there anything? A hair? A fingerprint?'

'A lot of people called on Janine. Trying to sort out all the evidence is a nightmare.'

'What about the appointments book?'

'There isn't one. That's disappeared.'

'It must have been someone pretty powerful who threw her off the pier.'

'Not necessarily,' said Jimmy. 'We've found threads of her white dress in the pier rail where she went over and bruises on her ankles. It looks almost as if someone pointed down at the water and said something like, "What can that be down there?" Janine leans over. The rail is quite low. Someone grasps her ankles and just tips her over.'

'It must have been someone who knew she couldn't swim.'

'Yes, that's what made us sure it was the husband.'

'What I would love to find out,' said Agatha, twiddling with the stem of her glass, 'is if there is anything in the background of any of them, I mean the people at the hotel, that would cause them to commit murder.'

'We've gone into that pretty thoroughly. Mary and Jennifer are a couple of single ladies who seem to have led boring and respectable lives. Daisy and Harry, the same. The colonel had a hard-working career in the army.'

'Northern Ireland?'

'Yes, like everyone else, but if you're starting to think about some sinister plot by the IRA, remember it wasn't the colonel who was murdered.'

'Why would anyone kill Francie and then her daughter?' said Agatha, half to herself. 'The pair of them must have got to know a great deal about their clients. Maybe they got to know something they shouldn't and tried a bit of blackmail.' She brightened. 'I'm sure that's it. Now if it was the husband, he might know what it was, and if he isn't saying anything, it might be information he's keeping back to use himself.'

The inspector looked at her fondly. 'You're as good as a book, Agatha. But Cliff, despite his appearance, is a weak creature. He was bullied by his wife, from all accounts. It was her work that kept him and she never let him forget it. Janine changed her will right after her mother's death. We've just found that out.'

'So Cliff does get the lot.'

'On the contrary. He was left nothing. Everything goes to the Spiritualist Society of Great Britain.'

'Blimey. So what's Cliff going to do for money?'

'Probably go back to working on the fairgrounds, which is where Janine met him.'

Agatha sat silent for a moment. Then she said, 'That's it!'

'That's what?'

'The reason for the missing money. Janine and Francie were gypsies, and gypsies do not like paying the tax man. There must have been a hell of a lot of money in Francie's box. Cliff must have taken it.'

'But Cliff didn't know about the changed will, or so he says, and Janine was still alive when Francie was murdered, so I don't follow your line of reasoning, Agatha.'

Agatha's face fell. 'Neither do I, now I come to think of it.'

He patted her hand. 'Let's talk about something more pleasant. I'm taking the day off on Sunday. Would you like to go for a drive?'

'Yes, that would be nice. Where?'

'Just along the coast. Stop somewhere at a pub for lunch.'

'I'd love to.'

'I'll pick you up at ten.'

After Agatha said goodbye to him, she walked into the hotel and looked into the lounge. They were playing Scrabble over by the fire, the group illuminated by the soft light from an old-fashioned standard lamp with a fringed shade, all of them crouched over the Scrabble tiles on the low coffee-table. The furniture in the lounge was heavy and Victorian, upholstered in dark green velvet. The velvet curtains of the same colour were closed over the long windows to shut out the night. Had they all subconsciously decided to shut out the world by not talking about it? Agatha had never even heard them discuss anything in the newspapers except for a few brief remarks about the coverage of the murder. Then, almost as if their heads were on pulled wires, they all turned their faces and looked at her. Agatha had an odd feeling that she was intruding on the meeting of some secret society.

Then Daisy called, 'Come and join us.'

Agatha shook her head, smiled and said goodnight.

As she undressed in her room, she began to speculate about a future with Jimmy. Mrs Jessop, she repeated to herself as she ran her bath. I could be Mrs Jessop and I will ask James Lacey to give me away. So there!

Sunday was a glorious day, all wind and glitter. It had rained heavily the day before and now everything was drying out in the sun. It was a yellow day, watery yellow sunlight shining in puddles and dancing on the choppy waves of the sea.

Agatha experienced a feeling of relief as they drove away from the hotel. In bad weather, as on the day before, the hotel became oppressive, like being locked away in a time warp. Although the others were friendly enough, the women no longer asked her advice on clothes or make-up and the colonel no longer seemed interested in outings to the theatre or anywhere else. The days are passing, thought Agatha as Jimmy drove his VW Polo along the coast road. I wonder if James Lacey misses me.

'So you haven't heard from her?' James Lacey was saying after church to Mrs Bloxby. 'And yet there's been another murder. I thought she might have come home to have a look at her cats. Then I thought she might have phoned me to consult me about the murders.'

'You haven't been exactly friendly with Mrs Raisin,' said Mrs Bloxby. 'Why don't you drive down and see her?'

'I might do that,' said James. 'Yes, I might just do that.'

After three hours' driving, he arrived at Wyckhadden and went straight to the Garden Hotel. He was told at the desk that Mrs Raisin had gone out and they did not know when she was expected back. 'Mrs Raisin?' said a tall, elderly man who had been passing the desk.

'Yes, Colonel,' said the manager. 'This gentleman is asking for Mrs Raisin.'

'Gone out with her boyfriend,' said the colonel. 'That inspector.'

James Lacey did not wait. There was no point. Agatha had always been a damned flirt.

'So that's the real story of why we didn't get married,' Agatha was saying later over dinner. 'It wasn't just because my husband turned up at the wedding. I really think James didn't care for me at all.'

'I hate to say this, Agatha,' said Jimmy, 'but you're right. If he had really loved you, he would have married you when everything settled down.'

They had talked all day with an easy companionship. Agatha was beginning to think more and more that marriage to Jimmy might be pleasant. There had to come a point in life to put away immature dreams of love and settle for friendship.

She only wished she could stop playing scenes over and over in her head where James would be shocked and jealous when he learned of her forthcoming marriage.

As Jimmy drove slowly back to Wyckhadden, Agatha said, 'There's a fairground.'

In a field beside the road ahead of them was the fairground, the lights sparkling against the night sky. They had passed it on their road out but it had been silent and deserted.

'Want to take a look around?' asked Jimmy. 'It's probably crawling with Francie Juddle's relatives.'

'I like fairgrounds,' said Agatha.

'Then let's go.' He drove off the road and into the car park.

'Not many people.'

'Wrong time of year, and there was a terrible weather forecast.'

'I'm surprised it's open on a Sunday,' said Agatha as they walked between the booths.

'They are usually open. They do stay closed until late in the afternoon on a Sunday, the idea being that everybody's had time to go to church. What do you want to try? It's one of those old-fashioned fairs. Not much in the way of exciting rides.'

'There's a Ferris wheel,' said Agatha, pointing upwards. 'I'd like to try that.'

'It's late. Some of the things are closing already. But we'll try.'

The Ferris wheel was still operating. Jimmy paid for two tickets and they climbed into one of the seats. The man who had sold them the tickets fastened a safety bar across their chair.

'We're the only ones,' said Agatha. 'I wonder if he'll bother operating it.' They sat for about five minutes with nothing happening. 'Let's get off,' Jimmy was just saying when, with a jerk, the Ferris wheel started up. The wheel sent them climbing higher. 'The wind's getting strong,' said Agatha, clutching Jimmy's arm.

Then, when their chair lurched and swung to the top, the wheel suddenly stopped dead.

'They often do this,' said Jimmy, putting an arm around Agatha. 'It'll start up in a minute.'

A great gust of wind sent the chair rocking. Jimmy leaned over the edge. 'What's happening?' he shouted, but the increasing wind tore his words away.

Agatha clung on to him. A blast of icy rain hit her cheek. Ahead of her she could see the lights of Wyckhadden and then, as if a hand had drawn a great veil over the town, it was swallowed up in the approaching storm.

The chair they were sitting on began to bucket and lurch. Down below, the lights of the fairground were beginning to go off one by one. Then the lights on the Ferris wheel went out, leaving them stranded in the increasing ferocity and blackness of the storm.

Jimmy held Agatha close and said, 'I'm going to climb down. You stay here and hang on like grim death.' He loosened the protective bar in front of them and lifted it.

'Don't leave me,' shouted Agatha.

'I've got to get down.' He shrugged off his coat and then kicked off his shoes.

He swung himself out of the chair and began to climb down the struts of the Ferris wheel. Agatha leaned over to try to watch him but the chair gave another huge lurch and she screamed and hung on with both hands.

What a way to die, she thought miserably. She wanted to drag Jimmy's coat over her but was frightened to loosen her grip on the chair. She prayed desperately, the soldier's prayer. 'Dear God, if there is a God, get me out of this!'

She was now drenched to the skin. How long since Jimmy had started to climb down? Ten minutes? An hour?

Why hadn't she worn gloves? Her fingers were becoming numb. What if she couldn't hold on any longer? She raised one hand and struggled to find the bar and fasten it back in front of her but the swaying of the chair was so violent that she gave up the attempt.

Oh, James, wailed her mind, will I ever see you again? What will happen to my cats?

And then she felt herself falling and let out a long wail of terror.

But then her panic receded. The Ferris wheel was starting to move. Down and down she went. Blue lights were beginning to flicker along the coast road. Jimmy had a mobile phone in the car. He must have called for help.

At long last the Ferris wheel lurched to a halt and there was Jimmy with several fairground people. And suddenly the fairground was full of police cars and an ambulance.

'You're going straight to hospital,' said Jimmy.

'I'm all right,' said Agatha, through chattering teeth.

'You might be suffering from hypothermia.'

'What happened?'

'I'll let you know as soon as I can,' said Jimmy.

Chapter Six

Agatha awoke in hospital in Hadderton the following morning. The sleepy policewoman, Trul, was sitting beside her bed.

Agatha struggled up against the pillows. 'So what happened?' she asked.

'The man operating the Ferris wheel said it jammed and he went to get help.'

'What!' Agatha was outraged. 'I don't believe that for a moment. Inspector Jessop had to climb all the way down that Ferris wheel in a storm because we were up there for ages.'

The policewoman rose. 'Now you're awake, do you feel strong enough to make a statement?'

'I feel fine. What's the medical verdict?'

'You were not suffering from hypothermia but you may be suffering from shock. I'll get Detective Sergeant Peter Carroll. He's outside.'

Carroll came in. 'Now, if you will begin at the beginning and tell me in your own words what happened,' he said, drawing out a notebook.

'I'm hardly likely to tell you in anyone else's words,' said Agatha crossly. She described succinctly how the Ferris wheel had stopped when they were right at the top. 'Before the storm blotted everything out,' said Agatha, 'I could see the lights in the fairground below going out. To me it looked as if they were packing up for the night and going to leave us up there.'

'That will be all for the moment,' said Carroll, closing his notebook.

'Can I leave?'

'That's between you and the hospital.'

'Then send in a nurse!'

When Carroll had left and had been replaced by a nurse, Agatha said she wanted to sign herself out. There was a long wait for a doctor and then all the forms to sign before her still-damp clothes were produced. They might at least have dried them, thought Agatha huffily.

She went out of the hospital, where steady rain was falling, and waited for the cab she had ordered. She began to feel very weak and shaky but she was determined to get back to the hotel. She took out the tranquillizers they had given her and threw them in a waste bucket beside the hotel entrance. In Agatha's experience, all tranquillizers did was delay shock and misery.

The cab arrived and she was driven the short distance to the hotel in Wyckhadden. She went straight up to her room and ran a hot bath, stripped off her clothes, and soaked in it, wondering all the while if some of Francie's relatives were responsible for her death and had tried to get the inspector out of the way. But she decided, as she towelled herself dry, that did not make sense. The fairground people must know that had Jimmy been killed, then they would have been plagued with police investigations until the end of time, not to mention a charge of manslaughter.

She realized she was hungry and it was lunch-time. She went down to the dining-room.

The rest were just finishing their meals. 'We were looking for you last night,' the colonel called over.

'I was nearly killed,' said Agatha. She told them about her adventure on the Ferris wheel, half expecting them to shy away from the subject, but they all came crowding around her table, demanding details.

'Probably revenge,' said the colonel when Agatha had finished.

'For what?'

'Oh, I remember when Jessop was in charge of a crackdown on that fairground, charged them with gluing down the coconuts on the shy and bending the sights of the rifles.'

Agatha felt disappointed. 'I had hoped their behaviour might have had something to do with the murders.'

'*Titanic* is showing at the cinema in Wyckhadden,' said the colonel. 'We all thought of going.'

'Why not?' said Agatha wearily. This lot were never going to discuss the murders and the idea of losing herself in a long film and forgetting about mayhem and murder was tempting. 'When did you plan to go?'

'We're going to the matinee. Special rates for old age pensioners.'

'That leaves me out,' said Agatha tartly.

'If you say so,' remarked the colonel, and Agatha looked at his old face quickly for signs of malice but it showed nothing.

Left to eat, Agatha carefully sliced a line down the middle of her plate and ate half. Once, in an attempt to up-market her reading, she had read Muriel Spark's *A Far Cry From Kensington*. In it, the heroine had figured out that if she ate only half of everything on her plate, she would lose weight. That had struck Agatha as being eminently sensible and she was hardly likely to starve, a half of the hotel's portions being the equivalent of any other hotel's full meal.

She was just finishing her coffee when old Harry popped his head round the door and said they were ready to leave. Agatha was travelling in one taxi with Harry and Daisy, the colonel in the one in front with Mary and Jennifer.

On the way, Daisy squeezed Agatha's arm and whispered, 'Come to my room later. I must speak to you.' Agatha nodded. At last! A crack in the silence.

The cinema was in the middle of the promenade and packed with old people. To Agatha's surprise, a haze of cigarette smoke was drifting in front of the screen. By all that was holy, a cinema which still allowed smoking. She was fumbling in her bag for her cigarettes when she realized with a sort of wonder that she had not smoked once or thought of it while she was out with Jimmy. She kept her handbag firmly closed and concentrated on the screen, which was showing advertisements for local businesses.

The film was one of those ones the Americans ruin by insisting on putting 1990s values on to historical events. The hero was miles too young to interest Agatha. But the special effects were stupendous. In fact, Agatha could swear, just as the *Titanic* hit that iceberg, that she could feel the water lapping around her feet. Then there were shouts and curses. There *was* water lapping about her feet.

'Must be an exceptionally high tide,' Agatha heard the colonel say. 'We'd better leave by the back door.'

The audience were filing out, apart from a few stalwarts who had put their feet up on the seat in front. The film was still running. They all filed outside into the pouring rain.

'Let's have a look at the sea,' said Jennifer. 'We're all wet anyway.'

They walked down a side street towards the promenade. Huge waves were crashing on to the promenade and sweeping up the street.

'Does this often happen?' asked Agatha.

'Every so often,' said Mary. 'It's a wonder the foundations of that cinema haven't been removed.'

They made their way to the hotel around the back streets. 'Will the hotel be flooded?' asked Agatha.

'The sea is never so ferocious along at the pier,' said Harry, 'and the staff always put out sandbags.'

They walked down a side street leading to the hotel. 'Look at that!' cried Agatha as a huge wave crashed right over the dance hall at the end of the pier. 'Surely it can't withstand a battering like that.'

'Tide'll be turning soon,' said the colonel.

Sure enough, sandbags had been piled up in front of the hotel. Agatha went up to her room to change into dry tights and shoes. How very British we all are, she thought as she dried her feet. No one demanded their money back. I bet no one's even written to the newspapers suggesting the cinema should be located at the back of the town. No, all they'll say is, 'We often have weather like this. It doesn't last long. Mustn't grumble.'

There was a knock at the door. Agatha put on a pair of slippers and opened it. Daisy stood there. 'Oh, you wanted a word with me,' said Agatha eagerly. 'Do come in.'

Daisy came in and closed the door behind her. She sat down in a chair by the window. 'Such dreadful rain,' she murmured.

'Would you like tea or something?' asked Agatha.

'No, I just want to talk.'

Agatha sat on the bed. 'So talk, Daisy.'

Daisy looked out again at the pouring rain. 'Did you enjoy the film?'

'All right until we got washed out. Is that what you wanted to discuss? The film?'

'No, no, of course not.' Daisy plucked nervously at her skirt. She's a bag of nerves, thought Agatha. It must be something about the murders.

Agatha waited patiently. Then Daisy said, 'You went off for a drink with the colonel last night.'

'I did not,' said Agatha crossly. 'Last night I was freezing to death at the top of a Ferris wheel.'

'I'm sorry. I forgot. Of course, it was the evening before that. I saw you go off with the colonel.'

'We went for one drink, that's all.'

Daisy clasped her hands and looked beseechingly at Agatha. 'Are you keen on him?'

'Colonel Lyche? No, frankly. Too old for me.'

'But why did you go off with him?'

'I wanted to ask him about the murders. Look here, Daisy, I find it most odd that there have been two murders committed and yet none of you ever want to discuss them.'

'Murder is not a thing ladies discuss,' said Daisy primly.

Agatha looked at her in exasperation. 'Is that really all you wanted to talk to me about? I mean, to warn me off the colonel.'

'I never –'

'I mean,' said Agatha, her tone softening, 'you are keen on the colonel and you thought I might take him away from you.'

'Yes.'

'Well, the colonel has no interest in me whatsoever.'

'But I saw you walking on the pier and he took your arm.'

'He's a gentleman. It was a gentlemanly thing to do. That's all. How long have you been keen on the colonel?'

'Years,' said Daisy sadly.

'Have you ever thought of asking him out for a drink?'

'Oh, no, I couldn't!'

'Why?'

'Ladies don't.'

'This is the nineties. They do now,' said Agatha. 'Look, that Gilbert and Sullivan company has moved to Hadderton. You could get a couple of tickets and say they were given to you by a friend, and would he like to use the other ticket?'

'I'll try that,' said Daisy, her eyes shining.

'Do you ever read any magazines?' asked Agatha curiously.

'Yes, I read newspaper supplements and sometimes *Good Housekeeping*.'

'Not *Cosmopolitan*?'

'No. Why?'

'Just wondered,' said Agatha, who had been thinking about all the raunchy articles on sex that appeared in women's magazines these days. 'Go for it, Daisy. At least you'll have an evening on your own with him.'

Daisy had just left when the phone rang. It was Jimmy, who said he was downstairs and would like to see her.

Agatha deftly applied a fresh coat of make-up, put on high heels instead of her slippers and made her way downstairs.

'How are you?' asked Jimmy with that warm smile of his which always lifted Agatha's heart.

'I don't seem to have suffered any damage at all,' said Agatha cheerfully. 'Although I do seem fated to get wet.' She told him about her visit to the cinema.

'Let's go into the lounge and have a drink,' said Jimmy. 'I took a look. No one's in there now.'

They walked in and sat down in front of the fire. 'I've got an exciting bit of news. Someone's turned himself in.'

'You've got the murderer!' The waiter appeared. Jimmy ordered drinks. When he had gone, Jimmy said, 'No, not the murderer. Some small-bit actor has confessed doing voices for Francie and Janine. They would describe the sort of voice they wanted. We found a pretty elaborate sound system in a lock-up that Francie had rented on the outside of the town.'

'Has he been charged?'

'Yes, with conspiracy to defraud. But he'll probably just get a fine. He didn't really know he was doing anything wrong and he needed the money. He works for a repertory company over at Hadderton.'

'Did he know them well? I mean, can he shed any light on why someone would want to kill both of them?'

'I'm afraid not. He's quite old. Been doing bits for them on and off for years. He said he needed the money and as far as he was concerned, seances are only another form of theatre.'

'I keep thinking and thinking about it,' said Agatha. 'So many unanswered questions. To go back to the first murder, why was Francie's door unlocked? Did you ask Cliff about that?'

'He says he doesn't know anything about it,' said Jimmy. 'But this is usually a very safe town.' He grinned. 'Or rather, it was before you came along. A lot of people don't bother locking their doors.'

'Yes, but I can't help feeling Francie must have been up to something to get herself murdered. And she had cash in that box.'

'You forget. She really did have a reputation as a witch in this town. Normally no one would have dared to go near her.'

Agatha frowned. 'There's something else that keeps nagging away at the back of my mind. Wait a bit. I've got it! When you first told me that Francie kept records and you described what that lot at the hotel had consulted her about, you said that Jennifer of all people had asked for a love potion.'

'Yes. So?'

'But this is *Jennifer* we're talking about. She's practically married to Mary. Why would she want a love potion? Did you ask her?'

'No, I didn't,' he said slowly.

'I wonder if she'd tell me,' said Agatha.

'Let's talk about us.' Jimmy put his hand over Agatha's. 'When this is all over, I don't like the idea of you disappearing out of my life.'

'Well, I'll come back and see you.'

'I was thinking of something more permanent.'

Agatha thought longingly of James Lacey. *He* should have been holding her hand and suggesting something more permanent.

'Can we leave it a bit longer, Jimmy? I'm very fond of you, but I feel I need a little more time.'

'We'll take it easy, then.' Jimmy turned slightly pink. 'It's not because of my failure to . . .'

'No, no,' said Agatha quickly. 'You'll find that side of things comes back easily.'

'Have you had a lot of experience?' he asked wistfully.

'Hardly any,' said Agatha, 'but women talk to each other the way men don't.'

'Then that's all right then. By the way, that girl who savaged your coat was charged.'

'What did she get?'

'Sixty days community service and ordered to pay fifty pounds compensation.'

'What! That coat cost a mint.'

'I'm afraid the magistrate, Mrs Beale, is a vegetarian and does not approve of fur coats. You can pick your coat up at the police station.'

Agatha shuddered. 'I don't want to see it again. You can have it, Jimmy. Give it to some charity.'

'I had a look at it. All it needs is the paint cleaned off and the slashes sewn up.'

'Not worth it. Someone else would probably have a go at me. That coat did mean a lot to me once. I saved and saved for it.'

'You could always use the fur to line a coat.'

'No, you have it. Give it away.'

'All right. What about Sunday? I don't know if I can get the time off with all this murder. But now the super's in charge, I'm taking a back seat.'

'Doesn't that bother you?' asked Agatha curiously.

'No, these things happen in a big case like this. With all the press breathing down our necks, I'm glad in a way not to be totally responsible for solving the case. I'd better be getting back.'

Agatha walked down to the promenade. The tide had receded. She walked to the sea-wall and looked over. The shingly beach was a mess of driftwood and debris: Coke cans, plastic cups, plastic wrappers, and even less savoury items of modern civilization, as if the whole sea had regurgitated all the unnatural mess on the beach.

And picking its way through the debris came a battered-looking white cat. Was that Francie's cat? Agatha made her way to a flight of stone steps leading down to the beach.

The cat came towards her and stopped. It was painfully thin and its white fur was matted and dirty.

'Oh, you poor thing,' said Agatha. She crouched down and held out her hand. 'Kitty, kitty.'

The cat gave a dry, rusty mew. Agatha tentatively stroked the wet fur.

Then she gathered the cat up in her arms and headed for the hotel.

Mr Martin met her as she walked into the reception area and said severely, 'No pets allowed.'

'It's only for a little while,' said Agatha defensively. 'Look, I'll make sure it doesn't mess anything and I'll pay the full hotel bill.'

Mr Martin hesitated. He had been regretting his offer to pay her bill in compensation for the coat. And now, with this second murder, who knew when Agatha Raisin would leave?

'Very well,' he said. 'But do tell the others this is a one-off situation.'

Agatha carried the cat up to her room. She picked up the phone and ordered milk and a dish of canned tuna fish.

When it arrived, the cat ate greedily. I'd better go out and get a litter tray and stuff, thought Agatha.

She went down to reception and asked for the name of a car-rental company, and having secured it, ordered a taxi which drove her to the car-rental firm. She chose a small black Ford Fiesta, drove into the centre of the town and asked around for the whereabouts of a pet shop and was told there wasn't one, but that she could get most things at the supermarket. She bought cans of pet food, a litter tray, bags of litter and a brush.

When she had carried all the stuff up to her room, it was to find the cat in the middle of her bed, busy washing itself. 'I wonder what you are called?' said Agatha. 'I'll have to call you something. And what am I going to do with you? I'll need to find a home for you. It's not fair on Boswell and Hodge if I take you home. And aren't you mild and friendly? Not at all like the horror who flew at me.' Talking away, she sat down and began to brush the cat, which stretched languidly and purred. 'I know, I'll call you Scrabble. I'll always think of Scrabble when I think of Wyckhadden.'

As she brushed the cat, Agatha's thoughts turned to Jennifer. How was she to get her alone? She always seemed to be with Mary.

The following day, it was Jennifer herself who offered the solution. She was alone, eating breakfast when Agatha walked into the dining-room.

'Where's Mary?' asked Agatha.

'Got a touch of migraine. She hasn't had one in ages. I've given her her pills. She'll have a bit of a sleep and then she'll be all right.'

'Mind if I join you?'

'Please.'

Agatha sat down. 'You're in the morning papers,' said Jennifer. 'All about you getting trapped on that Ferris wheel. The fairground people are sticking to their story that the wheel got stuck.'

Agatha walked over to the sideboard where the morning papers were spread out and picked up the *Hadderton Gazette*. She carried it back to the table and scanned the news item.

'They make light of it,' said Agatha, putting the paper down. 'Jimmy had to climb down from the top in that storm. He could have slipped and been killed. I could have frozen to death.'

'They're all frightened of the gypsies around here,' said Jennifer. 'The police usually don't do much. Jimmy Jessop was the only one who occasionally went after them. They'll probably get off with it. Some safety inspector will look at the Ferris wheel and then they'll get a smack on the wrist and told to be more careful, that's all. Agatha, I wonder if you'd come to Marks with me. There's a trouser suit I want you to look at.'

'That'll suit me fine. I'm not doing anything this morning.'

After breakfast, they set out in Agatha's car. 'I got fed up with walking in the rain and getting taxis,' said Agatha.

She drove into the central car park, which was next to Marks and Spencer.

'It's over here,' said Jennifer, leading the way through brightly coloured racks of clothes.

Agatha put her head on one side. 'No, I don't think so. Very smart. But rather masculine. I mean ... maybe you like things masculine.'

'Not really. But I'm not a pretty person and I'm old.'

'Like to try something new?'

'Anything to brighten me up.'

Agatha chose a fine black wool skirt, a soft-yellow silk blouse and a long black velvet waistcoat. 'I see you've been letting your hair grow a bit,' said Agatha. 'Suits you, a bit longer. And ... er ... if you don't mind me saying it, you're getting a bit hairy.'

'What do I do about that? Go back to Jerome?'

'No, we'll go to Boots and buy a depilatory.'

But as they walked out of Marks, Agatha saw a poster in Wyckhadden's one expensive department store advertising the services of a make-up consultant. 'Let's try that. I could do with some advice myself,' said Agatha.

After an hour, with a bag of new cosmetics each and newly painted faces, they went to the store restaurant for lunch. Agatha looked at the non-smoking signs and sighed. The very sight of them made her long for a cigarette.

'Never been interested in any men?' asked Agatha bluntly. Jennifer paused, a forkful of salad half-way to her mouth.

'One is from time to time,' she said frostily. 'I'm not a lesbian, you know.'

Agatha decided to take the bull by the horns.

'It was just that someone said something about you ordering a love potion from Francie.'

Jennifer chomped angrily on her salad and then said, 'I suppose by someone, you mean that inspector of yours.'

'Well, yes.'

'The police have no right to go about gossiping with everyone and anyone.'

'I'm a close friend of Jimmy's. It just came out.'

'I suppose there's no harm in telling you. We get visitors at the hotel in the summer and at Easter. There was this retired doctor, very charming, a widower. We used to go for walks. I was frightfully keen on him. I could see the end of his stay approaching and I felt I would do anything to make him take a deeper interest in me.'

'Did it work?'

'I never got a chance to find out. I'd confided in Mary. To my horror, she told him about it, made a joke of it. "Better watch what you drink," that kind of thing. He was terribly embarrassed.'

'I'm not surprised,' said Agatha faintly.

'He left the next day without saying goodbye. I had a terrible scene with Mary and she broke down and cried and said she was frightened of losing me, so I had to forgive her. We've been together so long.'

'Good heavens,' said Agatha. 'I'd never have thought it of Mary. I mean – forgive me – I thought you were the one that kept Mary away from people. I mean, she told me that she never made any friends at work because you were always waiting for her.'

'That's not true!' Jennifer poked at a piece of lettuce on her plate. 'How do these things happen, Agatha? I've never been an attractive woman. When I took care of Mary during her breakdown, she was so pathetically grateful. She said I had brought her back to life. No one had ever appreciated me before. I knew she was really very clever, not like me. She was – is – one of those all-round clever people who can turn their hand to anything. She was a good computer programmer. But people in her office didn't like her, and that's the truth.'

'Why?'

'I went to an office party once and one of the men told me that I should get Mary to stop plotting and planning. Although she's very clever, Mary really had no confidence in herself, and so she always was afraid she'd lose her job, so if anyone bright came along, she would spread gossip, little poisonous things, near enough the truth to damage.'

'But why didn't you leave her?'

'She wants me, she needs me, and no one else does. I think if I left her, she'd kill herself and I couldn't have that on my conscience. I'm sorry I got so angry with you over the Joseph Brady business, but Mary told me you forced her into it and then told her she was silly.'

'I said nothing of the sort!'

'I believe you,' said Jennifer on a sigh. 'She won't like us having gone out together, so she'll start telling me, and the others, little things about you. She's already told Daisy that you've been trying to get your claws into the colonel.'

Agatha leaned back in her chair and stared at Jennifer. 'And I thought you were all such friends!'

'We're more like relatives. We haven't really got anything but each other and we're all old. You've landed in an old folks' home, Agatha.'

'The other thing that bothers me,' said Agatha, 'is that none of you talk about the murders. Why?'

'Do you think I ought to have the chocolate cake for dessert?'

'Why not? You're slim enough. You haven't answered my question, Jennifer.'

'Oh, that. I think we feel we shouldn't talk about it.'

'Bad form?'

'That's an excuse. No, it's because we're all pretty sure one of us did it.'

Agatha stared at her, but Jennifer was calmly ordering chocolate cake. 'What about you, Agatha?'

'May as well. If I can't smoke, I may as well have some comfort.'

The waitress left with their order.

'What makes you think it's one of you?' asked Agatha.

'Just a feeling.'

'Who do you think could possibly have done it? Who's strong enough?'

'It wouldn't take much strength,' said Jennifer. 'Just a lot of rage and fright.'

'What about Mary?'

'I think if Mary had done it, she would have broken down and told me.'

'The colonel?'

'Perhaps. But what reason?'

'Daisy?'

'Too silly and weak.'

'Harry?'

'Oh, here's our cake.' Agatha waited impatiently until the waitress had left.

'I was asking you about Harry.'

'Could be. He's got a vicious temper. He believed all that stuff about her conjuring up the spirit of his dead wife, but then Francie slipped up. She got a bit carried away with her success because Harry was a regular visitor. Francie began to embroider too much. She had Harry's wife tease him about always losing socks. Now, Harry is a sock fanatic. He buys pairs of black socks, never a colour, and has always kept them in neat pairs. So he asks the spirit, "What about my red pair?" and the spirit answers that the red pair probably got lost in the wash. So Harry tries a few more trick questions. He reported Francie to the police as a fraud and her place was raided but they couldn't find anything. Harry made such a song and dance about it before he went to the police that someone must have tipped Francie off. He said he would kill her.'

'But *Harry*!' Agatha conjured up a picture of Harry with his dowager's hump and his tortoise-like face.

'He's got powerful arms,' said Jennifer, calmly forking cake.

'But Daisy believed in the seance.'

'At first. But not any more.'

'So why on earth did she send me to Francie?'

'Probably because despite her fake seances, Francie had a good reputation for cures.'

'Do you think it was one of you, Jennifer?'

She shrugged. 'To tell the truth, I can't really believe that – except when I think about Mary breaking up the seance, when I think we were all probably the last to see her alive, Janine that is.'

'It is usually the husband,' said Agatha. 'I don't suppose the police will expect us to hang around Wyckhadden for much longer. I would like to get home.'

'Away from your police inspector?'

'I'll probably be back to see him,' said Agatha, waving to the waitress. 'Shall we go?'

Agatha returned to her room and fed Scrabble and put down a bowl of water. The cat ate and then stretched and purred and curled about

Agatha's legs. 'I should really go home as soon as possible, Scrabble,' said Agatha. 'But what am I going to do with you? Cliff must be a murderer to turn you out.'

There was a knock at the door. Agatha opened it. Mary stood there. 'Come in,' said Agatha.

'Oh, you've got a cat,' said Mary. 'Isn't that Francie's cat?'

'I found it wandering on the beach, half starved.'

Mary closed the door and sat down.

'You spent a lot of time with Jennifer today,' she said brightly.

'Yes. How's your headache?'

'Fine, thank you. These new migraine pills are great. Why were you and Jennifer away so long?'

'Surely you asked her.'

'She's in a bad mood and the whole room smells of depilatory. She told me to mind my own business. Now that is not like Jennifer. I hope you are not coming between us, Agatha.'

'I don't get this,' said Agatha. 'You gave me the impression that it was Jennifer who was possessive, and yet here you are like the rejected lover accusing me of taking her away from you.'

'We have a special friendship,' said Mary huffily. 'I was surprised, that's all. I mean, it was Jennifer who said you were a pushy sort of woman and not really our sort.'

A vision of the Birmingham slum in which she had been raised loomed up in Agatha's mind. She banished it with an effort and said calmly, 'I must ask Jennifer what she meant by that.'

Mary gave a thin little laugh. 'She probably won't remember. To tell the truth, she's been losing her short-term memory.'

'Which means you just made it up. Please leave, Mary, I have to get ready for dinner.'

Mary got to her feet and made her way to the door. 'Do you know what I think?' she said.

'No, and I don't want to.'

'I think you knew all along about Joseph from your inspector friend and only pretended to help me to humiliate me.'

'That's not the sort of thing I would dream of doing,' said Agatha, 'but it gives me a good insight into the workings of your mind. Take a good look at the other side of the door.'

I don't like her, thought Agatha. There is something badly wrong with that female. Or is there something badly wrong with Jennifer as well?

The phone rang. Agatha answered to find a slightly breathless Daisy at the other end. 'Could you pop along to my room, Agatha? I need some advice. The colonel and I are going to the theatre tonight.'

'Which is your room?'

'Number five. Go along the corridor outside your door to the left and it's just around the bend.'

Agatha walked along to Daisy's room. It seemed a welter of dresses. 'I've been trying everything on,' wailed Daisy. 'It's turned very cold but I don't want to spoil a dress by wearing a cardigan over it.'

'Let's see.' Agatha rummaged through the pile of dresses on the bed. 'What about this?' She held up a smoky-blue wool dress.

'Oh, do you think so?' Daisy's face fell. She picked up a green sequinned gown. 'I thought something more dressy.'

'No, it would be too much. You don't want to frighten him off. Besides, all these green sequins will throw a green light up on your face and you don't want that. Put on the blue dress and let me see it. I think I've got the very thing to go with it.'

When Agatha returned, Daisy was wearing the blue dress. 'There,' said Agatha, handing her a deep-blue wraparound cape. 'You put it on like so. It's a bit like a poncho. You throw that end around your shoulders. There!'

'I like that,' said Daisy. 'You are good.'

'And you won't need a cardigan. That thing's very warm. Now let's tone down your make-up. Too much mascara. It's sticking your eyelashes together. And what happened to that new soft lipstick you got from Mr Jerome's wife?'

After dealing with Daisy, Agatha only had time for a hurried bath and change of clothes before going down to the dining-room. Old Harry was teasing the colonel and Daisy about their 'date'. But both Jennifer and Mary looked resentful, almost as if they guessed it was Agatha who had put the idea of Daisy's taking the colonel out into her mind.

Agatha carefully divided the food on her plate into half, à la Muriel Spark. It was delicious roast beef with Yorkshire pudding and little roast potatoes, courgettes, carrots, cauliflower cheese, new potatoes and peas. She felt again guiltily that half was the equivalent of a full meal anywhere else.

After dinner she felt restless and bored. 'Game of Scrabble?' suggested Harry.

'Why not?' said Agatha gloomily.

Mary and Jennifer joined them. No wonder I never guessed what feuds and passions and emotions were lurking under the surface, thought Agatha as Harry shook out the tiles. You would think I'd never had that confrontation with Mary.

She tried to concentrate on the game. A waiter came in and drew the thick curtains, shutting out the view of a small cold moon shining on a large cold sea. Where is Cliff, the husband, now? wondered Agatha. I must ask Jimmy. I wonder if I'll see him before the weekend.

After two games she excused herself and went up to her room to receive a rapturous welcome from Scrabble. 'You don't look at all like the fierce animal who attacked me,' said Agatha, stroking the cat's soft white fur. 'I hope Boswell and Hodge like you because I don't think I could bear to give you away.'

The phone rang after Agatha was undressed and climbing into bed. It was Daisy. 'Could you come along to my room, Agatha?'

Agatha said she would be along in a minute. She put on a dressing-gown and walked along to Daisy's room.

'How did it go?' she asked, sitting on Daisy's bed.

'We had such a nice time,' said Daisy, 'and he thanked me very much. I did suggest we might go somewhere for a drink afterwards but he said he was tired.' Her mouth drooped in disappointment.

'I should think a man like the colonel will feel honour-bound to repay the invitation,' said Agatha. 'He's been used to you as a friend. It will take time for him to think of you in any other light.'

'Oh, you are so right. I . . . I leaned against his arm in the theatre and he didn't draw away.'

Big fat deal, thought Agatha cynically. He probably didn't even notice. She said good-night to Daisy and went back to her room. An idea struck her. She picked up the phone and called reception. 'Are they still playing Scrabble?' she asked.

'Yes, they're in the lounge,' said the sleepy voice of the night porter.

'Colonel Lyche with them?'

'Yes, the colonel went upstairs and came back down and joined them.'

'Thank you.' Agatha put the phone down.

Poor Daisy.

Chapter Seven

The next few days were quiet for Agatha. With the exception of Daisy, the others seemed to be avoiding her. By Saturday, she found she was eagerly looking forward to Sunday, when she would see Jimmy again. She had phoned Mrs Bloxby and had asked if James had shown any signs of missing her. Mrs Bloxby had hesitated. She had heard from an angry James how he had driven to Wyckhadden, only to learn that Agatha had gone out with her inspector. Mrs Bloxby knew from Agatha's query that somehow the hotel had failed to tell her of James's call. She thought Agatha's inspector sounded nice and she had always thought James Lacey a dead loss, and so she begged the question by saying 'Well, you know what James is like,' which Agatha had interpreted to mean that James had shown no interest in her at all.

It would be nice to be Mrs Jessop, to be a married woman, one of a pair. She did not want to live out the rest of her life alone with her cats. So, instead of dashing back to

Carsely, she stayed on. She could simply have told the police she was going home. They had her home address and number. They could contact her any time they wanted.

On the Saturday, she went out for a walk. The day was bitter cold. The morning's frost had not melted. It glittered on the iron railings outside the hotel under a small red sun which stared down on the glassy sea behind a haze of cloud.

Agatha walked along the pier past the kiosks, closed for winter. Did Wyckhadden ever come to life in the summer, when a warm sun shone down and all the kiosks were open, selling buckets and spades, postcards and candy-floss? It was hard to imagine just such a day when the biting cold seemed to have frozen everything into silence.

She saw the tall figure of the colonel standing by the rail where Janine had gone over, looking down into the water.

'Morning, Colonel.'

He turned round. 'Morning, Agatha. Snow forecast.'

Agatha stopped beside him. 'Odd place, Wyckhadden. Seems to get every sort of weather but warm sunshine.'

'We had a grand summer last year. I had to buy a fan for my room, it was so hot.'

'Hard to imagine.'

'You know,' said the colonel, 'I often imagine the summers of my youth when I'm standing here. Different world, a safer world.'

'No murders?'

'I suppose there were. Of course there were. But they didn't happen to people like us.'

I was once one of *them*, thought Agatha, and deep down inside I still am, but she remained silent, looking at the sea.

'I see you've rented a car,' said the colonel.

'Yes, I'm used to having one. Got a bit tired of walking everywhere.'

'Do you know, there's a place on the road between here and Hadderton that serves hot scones and butter. Just the day for hot scones and butter,' said the colonel wistfully.

'I'm not doing anything,' said Agatha. 'Let's go.'

'Splendid!' He took her arm and they walked back along the pier. Agatha looked at the hotel. A brief flash of red sun on glass. She was sure again they were being watched through binoculars.

'Should we take any of the others?' she asked.

'Let's not bother,' said the colonel. 'I'll see them at lunch-time.'

They got into Agatha's car. Following the colonel's directions, she headed out on the Hadderton road. 'It's not far from here,' said the colonel at last. 'There it is up on the crest.'

'It's a farmhouse,' said Agatha.

'They serve teas and things.'

Agatha's small car lurched up the track leading to the farm. 'There seems to be more frost here than in Wyckhadden,' she said, looking at the white fields.

'Bit warmer down by the water, but not much.'

'And is there really snow in the forecast?' asked Agatha, stopping in front of the farmhouse.

'Cold front from Siberia.'

'There's always a cold front from Siberia,' grumbled Agatha. 'I wish they'd keep their cold fronts.'

'The reason they send them down to us,' said the colonel, 'is because they know we like to grumble about the weather. It's the favourite British topic of conversation.'

'Safer than murder, anyway,' said Agatha.

They got out of the car. An elderly lady answered the door to their knock. 'Why, Colonel. It's a while since we've seen you,' she said.

'Mrs Raisin, may I present Mrs Dunwiddy. Mrs Dunwiddy, Mrs Raisin.'

Agatha shook hands with her. Mrs Dunwiddy had neatly permed grey hair, a wrinkled face and bright, unusually blue eyes, very blue, sapphire-blue.

'Take Mrs Raisin straight through to the parlour. You know the way,' said Mrs Dunwiddy. 'There's a good fire.'

Agatha followed the colonel into a cosy room which was like something out of a tourist brochure: low beamed ceiling, horse brasses, chintz, Welsh dresser with blue-and-white plates, log fire crackling in an ancient ingle-nook fireplace. The room was obviously used as a small restaurant. There were five tables surrounded by Windsor chairs. They hung up their coats on pegs in the corner.

'Splendid!' said the colonel, rubbing his hands. 'You can even smoke here, Agatha.'

And before she knew quite how it had happened, Agatha had taken out a packet of cigarettes and lit one up.

Rats, she thought, here I go again. But she did not stub the cigarette out.

Mrs Dunwiddy came in and placed a covered dish on the table along with a plate of strawberry jam, a dish of butter and a bowl of thick yellow Devon cream. 'I'll bring the tea,' she said.

'How did you find this dream of a place?' asked Agatha.

'One summer. That's when I go for really long walks. Got to keep fit. Just happened on it.'

Mrs Dunwiddy brought the tea in, a fat china teapot decorated with roses, smiled at them and left.

'I'll never eat lunch after this,' said Agatha, lifting the dish and looking down at a pile of warm scones.

'It's nice to get away from the hotel once in a while,' said the colonel.

Agatha looked at him curiously. 'Don't you lot ever get fed up with each other?'

'Us at the hotel? I suppose we do. But no one wants to be alone in their old age and I suppose we've formed ourselves into a sort of family.'

'It's a strange set-up, or maybe it's these murders that make it seem strange. Did you enjoy your evening at the theatre?'

'Yes, very much. Jolly kind of Daisy to ask me.'

'She's good company,' said Agatha, determined to put in a good word for Daisy.

The colonel laughed. 'Daisy agrees with anything I say, which a lot of men would like, but my wife was a woman of very independent mind, rather like you, Agatha. I prefer the company of that sort.'

Damn, thought Agatha. Poor Daisy.

'I think Daisy is actually very shy and unsure of herself. I think she probably has a strong mind.'

'But clinging. She leaned on me all through the performance and she was wearing one of those sort of cloying perfumes. Quite claustrophobic.'

Agatha wondered if she could let Daisy have some of that love potion.

'I'm very fond of Gilbert and Sullivan,' said

the colonel. 'They're doing the *Pirates of Penzance* tonight. Care to go?'

'Just you and me?'

'Yes, if you would care to.'

Agatha hesitated. Then she said, 'Me being the visitor and outsider might upset some of the others. They might feel, well, excluded.'

'So they don't need to know.' The colonel buttered another scone.

'So how do we manage it?'

'I get the tickets . . . you want more of this cream?' Agatha shook her head. 'The show's at eight o'clock. You drive there. I take a cab and meet you outside.'

Agatha thought of another evening in the hotel. 'Okay, you're on,' she said.

Agatha put on a warm sweater, wool skirt and boots that evening. She felt that to really dress up for the colonel would, in a way, be another treacherous knife in Daisy's bosom.

Scrabble, the cat, had demolished two cans of cat food and was lying on the bed, purring sleepily.

'Be a good cat until I get back,' said Agatha. Scrabble opened one green eye and stared at her and then closed it again.

Agatha picked up her coat and went downstairs. Daisy was pacing up and down the reception area.

'Where are you going, Agatha?' she asked sharply.

'Out to meet Jimmy,' lied Agatha.

'The colonel has just gone out,' fretted Daisy. 'I asked him where he was going and he said he was going for a walk. I offered to accompany him but he said he was meeting an old army friend.'

'Nice for him,' said Agatha casually and made her escape.

She got in her car, switched on the engine and let in the clutch. She saw to her irritation that Daisy had come out on to the hotel steps and was watching her. Agatha drove off as if she were going into town, then she circled back and drove past the hotel. She swore under her breath. Daisy was still standing on the steps, and she stared at the car.

The colonel was waiting outside the theatre. They went in together. 'I got good seats. I think the cold has kept most people away,' he said.

The performance began. Agatha forgot about Daisy, forgot about murder and settled back to enjoy herself. But at the second interval, she turned and looked around the theatre. As she looked up at the dress circle, her eye was caught by the flash of blonde hair but the woman moved her head behind one of the gilt pillars. That's Daisy, thought Agatha, all her enjoyment in the evening leaving her. I'm sure that was Daisy.

During the last act, she turned and looked up but the seat next to the pillar was empty.

I must have imagined it. And why should I feel guilty? thought Agatha angrily.

When the colonel suggested they go for a drink after the performance, she agreed.

'This is fun,' said the colonel. 'Nice to have different company for a change.'

Agatha would have liked to discuss the murders but knew she would not get anything out of the colonel, so she told him about her life in the village and he told her army stories and they sat there amicably chatting until after closing time.

There *are* men in this world who find me good company, thought Agatha rebelliously. To hell with James Lacey.

She drove the colonel back and dropped him off before they got to the hotel. Before she want up to her room, she said to the night porter, 'I'm tired. I do not want any calls whatsoever put through to my room, not even calls from the residents of this hotel.'

The night porter made a note. Agatha scuttled up to the sanctuary of her room.

After ten minutes, there came a knocking at the door, followed by Daisy's voice, shouting, 'Agatha!'

Agatha pulled a pillow over her head, feeling guilty and threatened. After several more furious bouts of knocking, Agatha was at last left in peace.

In the morning, she breakfasted in her room, fed the cat, and then wondered if she could get out of the hotel without going through the main entrance. She phoned Jimmy and told him she would pick him up along the promenade outside the cinema.

'When?' he asked.

'About fifteen minutes.'

'Why? Press bothering you again?'

'No, I'll tell you about it when I see you.'

Agatha put on her coat and then opened her door and looked cautiously up and down the corridor. There must surely be a fire-escape somewhere.

She walked along silently round the corner, quickly past Daisy's room, past other rooms to the end. There it was, clearly marked. FIRE-ESCAPE. She pushed down the bar and opened the door. An iron fire-escape led down to the hotel gardens at the side. She could not shut the door from the outside. She would just need to leave it, closed as much as possible, but not locked, until she returned.

It was even colder than the day before and a chill wind whipped at the skirts of her coat as she made her way down. She scuttled around the side of the hotel and into her car and drove off without looking up at the hotel windows, frightened that she would see Daisy glaring out at her.

Jimmy's tall figure could be seen waiting outside the cinema. He got in the car. 'This is a very small car,' said Agatha apologetically. 'You'd better push that seat back a bit. Now, where do you want to go?'

'If you drive straight ahead, we can go along the coast a bit. I'd like to talk. What have you been up to?'

'Not behaving very well. No, I've been behaving all right, I think. No, I haven't.'

'Out with it, Agatha.'

'It's like this. If it weren't for you, Jimmy, I would sign off at the police station and go home.'

'What! You! The great amateur detective of the Cotswolds.'

'I'm not the great amateur detective of anywhere. Inspector Wilkes, you know, the one at Mircester, he was right when he said I didn't solve crimes, I just blundered about in people's lives until something happened.' She told him about Daisy and the colonel. She ended by saying, 'So you see, I was disloyal to Daisy. The colonel's not the slightest bit interested in her, but she doesn't know that. First I shatter Mary's dream and now I'm well on the way to shattering Daisy's. It was selfish of me. I was restless and bored and the colonel is good company.'

'Better than me?'

'No, nothing like that, Jimmy. He's a polite, elderly gentleman, that's all.'

There was a little silence and then Jimmy said, 'You are a very attractive woman, Agatha.

You should be very careful. Don't let Colonel Lyche fall in love with you.'

'I think that's highly unlikely, but it's nice of you to say I'm attractive, Jimmy.' Agatha privately did not think she was attractive at all. Attractive women were the anorexic ones you saw in the magazines with the glossy pouting lips. They were not stocky middle-aged women with small eyes.

'Now how do I make my peace with Daisy?' she asked.

'You could say you wanted to get the colonel alone to find out what he really thought of Daisy?'

'That might be raising false hopes. He actually doesn't rate Daisy very highly. I would need to lie.'

'Why don't you move out of that hotel and move in with me?'

Here was an opportunity to find out what life would be like with Jimmy. But she thought of that bright sterile bungalow up at the back of the town and repressed a shudder.

'Not yet, Jimmy. I'll stick it out a little bit longer. How's the case going?'

'It's going nowhere. The super doesn't agree with me. I think it's the work of a lucky amateur. I think in each murder, he or she saw the opportunity and took it.'

'But the murder of Francie was planned, surely. The money that was taken. I really don't think it can be any of them at the hotel,

Jimmy. I mean, the idea that one of them could murder Francie and then calmly sit and play Scrabble is beyond belief. And wait a bit, wait a bit! You say she wasn't murdered in the middle of the night?'

'No. Early in the evening.'

'So what was she doing in bed? She *was* murdered in bed?'

'Yes.'

'So she could have been waiting for a lover!'

'Could be. We're still trying to find out if there was anyone she was playing around with over in Hadderton.'

'Any sign of the murder weapon?'

'Not yet. But we're pretty sure now what was used.'

'What?'

'Cliff told us the other day that Francie always had one of those marble rolling-pins in the kitchen and it's gone.'

'Took his time about it.'

'He was only making a suggestion. I mean, it's not something that Cliff, or probably even Janine, would notice was missing.'

'What was he doing in the house?' asked Agatha. 'I thought he didn't inherit anything.'

'We took him back there and made him go through everything. It was my idea. I was sure it was in a way a murder committed out of fright and rage. The more I think about it, the more I am sure Francie had something on someone.'

'Blackmail?'

'It's possible, and it's possible her daughter knew who she was blackmailing.'

'That lot at the hotel all went to her, and Harry and Daisy knew her seances were a trick.'

'But you forget, Agatha, quite a lot of people in Wyckhadden went to her as well, including people from Hadderton who preferred her skills to her daughter's.'

Agatha sighed. 'I suppose it will end up one of those unsolved mysteries.'

'Something usually breaks. I've not had any experience of murder apart from that one case I told you about. But I've read about cases and heard about them from other police officers. Just when you think you're at a dead end, the murderer does something to betray himself.'

'Have that lot at the hotel all got alibis for earlier that evening, I mean the evening of Francie's murder?'

'None of them was seen leaving the hotel.'

'But the murder could have been committed in broad daylight!'

'Hardly. It gets dark at four-thirty in the afternoon.'

'Wait a bit,' said Agatha. 'I've just thought of something. When I left the hotel, I didn't want to run into Daisy and so I left by the fire-escape. It leads down the side of the building. Any of them could have gone that way and re-entered that way.'

'Oh, let's forget about it and enjoy the day.'

'We seem to have been driving through miles of bleak countryside. What's up ahead?'

'There's a pretty fishing-village called Coombe Briton, I'd like you to see. Only another couple of miles.'

Agatha drove on until she saw a sign COOMBE BRITON pointing to the right and swung off the main road and down a twisty road towards the sea.

It was a picturesque village with cottages painted pastel colours and narrow cobbled streets. 'There's an old inn down at the harbour,' said Jimmy. 'I thought we could have a drink there, go for a little walk and then have lunch.'

Agatha parked outside the inn and they walked inside to a low-raftered room. Agatha was disappointed. Everything inside had been done up in mock-Tudor: fake suits of armour, a bad oil painting of Queen Elizabeth over a fireplace where fake logs burned in the gas fire. But Jimmy seemed delighted with the place and told Agatha it was famous for its 'atmosphere'.

Agatha's dream of being an inspector's wife flickered and began to fade. She tried to remind herself that pre-James and pre-Carsely she would not have even noticed that this pub was in dreadful taste, and what was good taste anyway? But it did seem silly to have such a genuinely old pub and put fake things in it. A real fire blazing away would have been lovely. Then there were those friends of his, Chris and Maisie at the dance. If she married Jimmy, would she be expected to entertain people like that? Come on, she chided herself, Wyckhadden's a small town and it stands to reason that Jimmy's on nodding terms with most of the population.

'What are you thinking about?' asked Jimmy.

'I was remembering that couple at the dance, Chris and Maisie. Known them long?'

'Oh, yes. Chris was a police constable but he left the force. Does security for a factory over at Hadderton. He's a good friend. He and Maisie were a tower of strength when my wife died.'

They had a drink and then walked along the harbour. How the sea changed from one day to the next, marvelled Agatha. Today it was black with great white horses racing in to crash against the old harbour wall.

'Hope it doesn't snow before we get back,' said Jimmy, looking at the sky.

'Do you think it will? We haven't had a bad winter for ages.'

'Forecast's bad. Here, come against the shelter of the wall. I've got something to show you.'

Jimmy fished in the pocket of his coat and took out a small jeweller's box. 'Open it,' he urged.

Agatha opened it. Nestling in the silk inside was a ruby-and-diamond ring. She looked up at him, startled.

'I want to marry you, Agatha,' said Jimmy. 'Will you?'

Agatha forgot about the pseudo-pub, about Chris and Maisie. All she felt was a surge of gladness mixed with power that this nice man wanted her for his wife.

'May I put it on?'

And as shyly as a young miss, Agatha held out her left hand. Jimmy slipped the ring on. He bent and kissed her, his lips cold and hard. Agatha felt a surge of passion. Somewhere at the back of her mind a little superstitious voice was screaming that she had tricked Jimmy into this with a love potion, but she ignored it.

Arm in arm, they walked back to the pub for lunch. 'I ordered in advance,' said Jimmy.

The first course was Parma ham, like a thin slice of shoe leather on a weedy bed of rocket. The main course, billed as rack of lamb, turned out to be one minuscule piece of scragend of neck surrounded by mounds of vegetables, and was followed by sherry trifle – heavy sponge with no taste of sherry whatsoever. The old Agatha would have called for the manager and told him exactly what she thought of the food, but she was about to be Mrs Jimmy Jessop, and such as Mrs Jimmy Jessop did not make scenes. 'I have friends in

London,' said Agatha. 'Would you mind if I sent a notice of our engagement to *The Times*?'

He smiled at her fondly. 'I want the whole world to know about us, Agatha.'

So let James Lacey read it and let James Lacey make what he likes of it, thought Agatha defiantly.

'I hope you like cats,' she said. 'I've got three.'

'Three! But of course you've got to bring them.'

'I've a lot of furniture and stuff.'

'I'll leave it to you to redecorate,' said Jimmy.

So that's all right, thought Agatha.

They finished their meal and went out into a white blizzard. 'Damn,' said Agatha, 'I didn't notice any salt on the road as we came along.'

'I'll drive if you like,' said Jimmy.

'No, I'm a good driver,' said Agatha, who was actually a fair-to-middling driver but always liked to be in the driving seat, metaphorically and physically.

Getting out of the village was a nightmare. Going up the steep cobbled street, the wheels spun and struggled for purchase on the icy surface. 'Pull on the hand brake and change sides,' said Jimmy. 'I think I can manage.'

Agatha reluctantly surrendered the wheel and then wondered sulkily how Jimmy managed to urge the little car up that icy street when she had failed. When they reached the main coast road, it was to find a gritter had recently been along, although the road in front was whitening fast despite the mixture of grit and salt.

'I hope we make it to Wyckhadden,' said Jimmy, staring out into the blinding whiteness of the blizzard.

'I could drive now,' said Agatha.

'No, darling, better leave it to me.'

Now wasn't that just what every woman should like to hear? No, darling, leave it to me? But Agatha felt useless and diminished. Only the thought of that announcement appearing in *The Times* cheered her up.

'We won't be going far tonight,' said Jimmy, parking outside the hotel at last after a gruelling journey. 'I've got to go home and make a few calls. I must tell my children about our engagement. I'll come back for you later.'

'Can't I run you home?'

'No, it's safer to walk.' Jimmy got out and locked the car and as she came round, handed her the keys. He bent and kissed her. 'See you later,' he said, and hunching his shoulders against the blizzard, he hurried off.

Agatha went into the reception. Daisy came shooting out of the lounge as if she'd been on watch.

'I want a few words with you,' she began.

Agatha pulled off her glove and exhibited the engagement ring. 'Congratulate me!'

Daisy went quite white and put a shaking hand on to the reception desk to support herself.

'Yes, Jimmy has just proposed,' said Agatha brightly.

'Oh!' Colour began to appear in Daisy's cheeks. 'You mean your inspector. I am so very happy for you, Agatha. I thought . . . never mind.'

'What weather,' said Agatha cheerfully. 'Has it been like this before?'

'Sometimes. But it never lasts very long. Engaged! I must tell the colonel.'

Daisy tripped off. Agatha went up to her room and showed the ring to Scrabble. Then, taking out her credit card, she phoned *The Times* and arranged for the announcement of her engagement to be placed in the newspaper on the following morning.

After she had replaced the receiver, the phone rang. She picked it up. It was Jimmy. 'I'm afraid I've been called out, Agatha.'

'Anything to do with the murders?'

'No, something else.'

'How can they expect you to go out in weather like this?'

'They do. I'll call you when I'm through to say goodnight. You've made me a very happy man, Agatha. I love you.'

'Love you too, Jimmy,' lied Agatha. 'Hear from you later.'

She sat down suddenly on the bed and automatically stroked Scrabble's warm fur. 'I'll need to go through with it,' she said. 'I *want* to go through with it,' she added fiercely. 'I don't want to spend my old age alone.'

Then she decided to phone Mrs Bloxby. She told the vicar's wife the news. There was a little silence and then Mrs Bloxby said, 'Do you love him? I mean, are you in love with him?'

'No, but I think that will come.'

'And is he in love with you?'

'Yes, he is.'

'It can be very suffocating and guilt-making to be married to someone who is deeply in love with you and then find yourself faced daily with a love you cannot return.'

'I'm not a young thing any more,' said Agatha crossly. 'Love is for the young.'

Again that little silence and then Mrs Bloxby's voice came down the line. 'I am only saying this because I care for you. James will be upset, yes, but then it will pass and you will be married to a man you don't love. Never try to get even, Agatha. It doesn't ever work.'

'Jimmy is a good man and I am very fond of him and I will be delighted to spend the rest of my life with him,' said Agatha. 'I haven't thought about James once since I met him.'

'Will it be in the papers?'

'*The Times* tomorrow.'

'I don't think James is the sort of man to read the social column.'

But someone else in the village will, thought Agatha. And someone else will tell him.

She asked after her cats and about what was going on in the village and then rang off, feeling flat. 'I did not get engaged to Jimmy just to get revenge on James Lacey,' she told the cat fiercely. Scrabble gave her a long, studying look from its green eyes.

Agatha went down to dinner that evening to find that although it was freezing and snowing outside, the atmosphere inside had thawed towards her. Daisy had told them the news of her engagement and they all crowded around her table to admire the ring and congratulate her.

After dinner, the colonel suggested the usual game of Scrabble and they all gathered in the lounge just as all the lights went out.

'Power cut,' said the colonel. 'They'll be in with candles in a minute.'

They sat in front of the fire. Agatha thought the light from the flames flickering on their faces made them look sinister.

Two elderly waiters came in carrying not candles but oil-lamps. Soon the room was bathed in a warm golden glow.

'Very flattering light. You look quite radiant tonight, Agatha,' said the colonel. Daisy glared, little red points of light from the fire dancing in her eyes. 'In fact,' went on the colonel, 'I have always found that one wedding leads to another. Who's next? You, Harry?'

'Who knows?' said Harry. 'I may be lucky.'

Daisy smiled at the colonel coquettishly. He

quickly averted his eyes from hers and said, 'Let's get started.'

The newspapers were delivered in Carsely the following morning as usual, for the blizzard which was blanketing England on the south coast had not yet reached the Midlands.

James read his *Times* as usual but without reading the social column and then turned to the crossword. For some reason, Monday's crossword was usually easier than the rest of the week and to his disappointment he finished it in twenty minutes. Nothing left to do but get on with writing his military history. Then, like all writers, as he sat down at the computer, his mind began to tell him he ought to do something else first. He was nearly out of coffee. Of course he had enough to last the day but with the blizzard coming, it wouldn't do any harm to get in supplies.

He drove to Tesco's at Stow-on-the-Wold and found the car park almost full. A wartime mentality had hit everyone because of the approaching storm. People were trundling laden trolleys past him to their cars.

Infected by the shopping mania, he bought not only coffee, but a lot of other stuff he had persuaded himself he needed. He was just pushing his shopping trolley out to the parking area when he was stopped by Doris Simpson, Agatha's cleaner.

'Well, our Agatha's full of surprises,' said Doris.

James smiled down at her tolerantly. 'What's she got herself into now?'

'John Fletcher phoned me from the Red Lion just before I went out. It's in *The Times*.'

'What is?'

'Why, our Agatha's engagement. Someone called Jessop she's going to marry. Mrs Bloxby says he's a police inspector. Did you ever?'

'I knew that was on the cards,' lied James.

'There you are. I hope she gets married in Carsely. I like a wedding. Not that she can wear white. Miss Perry over at Chipping Campden got married the other week. Now she's about our Agatha's age. She wore rose-pink silk. Very pretty. And the bridesmaids were all in gold.'

'I must go,' said James. 'Snow's arrived.'

'So it has,' said Doris as a flake swirled down past her nose. 'Must get on.'

She can't do this, thought James. She's only doing it to get at me. I'll go down there and reason with her.

But by the time he got home, the flakes were falling thick and fast. He phoned the Automobile Association and found all the roads to the south were blocked.

Sir Charles Fraith was having a late breakfast with his elderly aunt. She put down the newspaper and said, 'Don't you know someone called Raisin? Didn't she come here?'

'Agatha Raisin?'

'Yes, that's her. It's in the paper.'

'What is?' asked Charles patiently.

'She's engaged to be married to some fellow called Jessop,' said his aunt.

'Fast worker, Aggie. I'll phone Bill Wong and see if he knows about it.'

Charles got through to Detective Sergeant Bill Wong at Mircester police. 'She's getting married!' exclaimed Bill. 'Who to?'

'Fellow called Jessop.'

'That'll be Inspector Jessop of the Wyckhadden police.'

'I thought Aggie was eating her heart out for James Lacey.'

'She must have got over it.'

'She's probably doing it to annoy him. I know Aggie. I'll go down there and put a stop to it.'

'You shouldn't, and anyway, you can't,' said Bill. 'The roads are blocked.'

'I should stop the silly woman. I bet she doesn't give a rap for this inspector.'

'She's over twenty-one.'

'She's twice over twenty-one,' said Charles nastily.

'Why don't you phone her? It said in the papers when they were writing about the murder that she was staying in the Garden Hotel.'

'Right. I'll do that.'

But the lines in Wyckhadden were down.

Agatha was never to forget the suffocating claustrophobic days that followed, immured in the hotel. No electricity. No phones. No television.

On the Wednesday morning, Agatha found Harry sitting alone in the lounge. 'Not even a newspaper,' he mourned. 'I've never known it as bad as this. And no central heating. You would think a hotel as expensive as this would have a generator. I'm bored.'

Agatha walked to the window. 'It's stopped snowing,' she said over her shoulder.

'Sky's still dark and more has been forecast,' said Harry, rising and joining her.

'We could build a snowman,' joked Agatha.

'Splendid idea.' To Agatha's surprise, Harry was all enthusiasm. 'Let's put on our coats and build one right outside the dining-room window where they can see it at lunch-time.'

Soon, well wrapped up, they both ventured out. The snow lay in great drifts. 'I'll go first,' said Harry. 'Clear a path.'

He headed to a spot in front of the dining-room window. Agatha, like Wenceslas's page, followed in his footsteps.

'I used to be good at this,' said Harry. 'I'll shape the base if you roll a snowball for a torso.'

'Where are the others?' asked Agatha.

'In their rooms, I think.' Harry worked busily.

'You never talk about the murders,' said Agatha.

'No, I don't. Nothing to do with me. Why should I?'

'You knew Francie. Had a seance with her.'

'Oh, that. Maybe that's one reason I don't want to talk about it.'

'Why?'

'Because she tricked me. I missed my wife dreadfully and I must have been crazy to go to her. Mind you, her potions and ointments seemed to work.'

'So what happened?' asked Agatha.

'I really thought it was my wife. That was until the voice that was supposed to be my wife told me that the bit about the eye of the needle in the Bible was true. Said I should give my money to Francie.'

'"But if a rich man can't enter the kingdom of heaven, how can a rich woman?" I asked.

'Ah, the voice said, Francie would send it on to a good cause. That's when I got suspicious. My wife was very thrifty. "Must save for our old age," that's what she always said. I reported Francie to the police. But I'd gone along with it for a little, been conned, and felt like a fool. Don't want to talk about the woman. She's dead anyway.'

Agatha rolled a large snowball, and with surprising strength in one so old, Harry lifted it on to the base he had formed while he was talking. 'Another one for the head,' he ordered.

He began to shape the torso into a woman's bust. Agatha watched, amazed, as a snow-woman began to take shape. 'Could you go to the games cupboard,' asked Harry, 'and get me two marbles for eyes? And some make-up for the face?'

'Right. What about hair?'

'Could you find something? Black hair? And do you have an old dress or coat or something?'

Perfectionist, thought Agatha. What happened to the old-fashioned snowman made of three balls of snow and with a carrot for a nose?

She went up to her room and found an Indian blouse which she had decided she did not much like. What to use for hair? He would need to make do with one of her scarves. She picked out a black one and then found a lipstick and blusher. She then went to the games cupboard in the lounge and took two blood-red marbles out of a jar.

Afterwards, as she surveyed Harry's handiwork, she wished she had taken out two blue or grey marbles, for the red effect was sinister. Harry had created a woman with staring red eyes in a snow face like a death mask. With the black scarf draped round her head and the Indian blouse fluttering in the wind, the snow-woman looked remarkably lifelike and ghoulish.

A gong sounded from the hotel. 'Lunch!' said Harry. 'Let's get to the dining-room before the rest of them. I want to see their reactions.'

They left their coats in the lounge and hurried into the dining-room.

Daisy, Mary, Jennifer and the colonel came in together.

The colonel stopped dead. 'By George,' he said. 'Would you look at that!'

Outside the window the red marble eyes glared in at them from the white face and the black scarf moved in the wind and the blouse fluttered. In that moment, Agatha realized the snow-sculpted features bore a remarkable resemblance to the dead Francie.

'Is it something out of a carnival?' asked Daisy.

But Mary uttered a moan, put a shaking hand to her lips and fainted dead away.

Chapter Eight

'The phones are still down,' said the colonel after lunch. Mary was lying down in her room being ministered to by Jennifer.

'I know,' said Agatha. 'I tried to phone Jimmy.'

Agatha was beginning to wonder why Harry had gone out of his way to make his snow figure so much like Francie. And why had he such ability?

'Thought that snow thing of Harry's was in remarkably bad taste,' said the colonel. He and Daisy and Agatha were sitting in front of the fire in the lounge.

'I'm amazed, however, at his expertise,' said Agatha. 'I thought he was going to make a traditional snowman.'

'I suppose once a sculptor, always a sculptor.'

'What! Harry?' Agatha had fondly imagined that sculptors, however old, would look, well, more bohemian.

'Haven't you ever heard of Henry Berry before?' asked the colonel. 'He was quite famous in his day. Doesn't do it any more. Says he hasn't the strength.'

'He seems remarkably strong to me.' Agatha remembered the ease with which he had lifted and shaped the heavy snow.

'Anyway, he gave poor Mary a dreadful fright,' said Daisy. She winked meaningfully at Agatha and then jerked her head slightly towards the door. Agatha correctly interpreted that to mean that Daisy wanted her to leave her alone with the colonel. But it had started to snow again and the rooms were cold because the central heating wasn't working. Scrabble was all right. She had placed a hot-water bottle on the bed wrapped in a towel and last seen, Scrabble had been comfortably coiled around it.

The manager came in with a portable radio. 'I thought you might like to hear the news,' he said, putting it down and switching it on. 'There is a thaw forecast for this evening. They hope to have electricity restored by this evening as well. Dear me, so much food wasted. We've had to throw a lot of stuff out of the freezers.'

The colonel cocked his head. 'Listen.'

The voice of the news announcer began a catalogue of disasters, of blocked roads and thousands of homes without power. Daisy shifted in her chair and looked at Agatha angrily. You can glare all you want, thought Agatha, but I am not leaving this warm fire.

She longed to be able to phone Jimmy and find out if there was anything sinister in Harry's background.

The colonel at last switched off the radio. 'Thank you, Mr Martin. It certainly seems as if there is a thaw coming.'

The manager took the radio away. 'I think I'll go to my room and get a book.' The colonel rose to his feet. Daisy watched him with hungry eyes as he left the lounge. She's getting worse, thought Agatha.

When the colonel had gone, Agatha said, 'I know you want me to leave you alone with him, Daisy, but I do not want to go upstairs and sit in a cold bedroom, and it's not as if I can go out for a walk.'

'I only wanted a few moments,' said Daisy sulkily.

Agatha leaned forward. 'If I can give you a bit of advice, Daisy, it's no good being so keen, so needy. It drives the gentlemen away. You'll frighten him off.'

'Are you speaking from personal experience?' asked Daisy nastily.

'Yes,' said Agatha, thinking of James Lacey. She had even pursued him to Cyprus and a fat lot of good that had done.

'You went out with the colonel,' accused Daisy. 'I saw you.'

'It *was* you. At the theatre.'

'Yes, and he took you out for a drink afterwards, which is more than he did for me.'

Agatha sighed. 'Look here, Daisy, the reason he felt comfortable with me was because he knows I'm not interested in him. What if he had seen you watching us? You know these potions of Francie's. I've got a bit of love potion left.'

'Did you get it to put in the colonel's drink?'

'No, I got it as a bit of a joke, but I'll let you have some.'

'Will it work?'

'Haven't you tried it before?' asked Agatha.

'I thought about it but I wanted him to love me for myself. But if you wouldn't mind . . .'

Agatha got to her feet. 'I'll get it before he comes back.'

She went up to her room and found the bottle. She must only use a few drops. She wanted to keep some for analysis, along with the hair tonic.

She went back to the lounge. 'Could you put it in for me?' whispered Daisy. 'I'm terrified I'll get caught.'

'Don't rush me,' admonished Agatha. 'I'll need to wait for the right moment.'

The right moment occurred that very afternoon when they were all gathered round the fire. 'Nothing to do but get drunk,' mourned the colonel. 'Care to join me in a bottle of claret, Harry?'

'Good idea.'

'When it arrives, create a distraction,' Agatha whispered to Daisy.

Agatha and the rest ordered coffee. Agatha slipped the bottle out of her handbag and into her hand.

The waiter came in carrying a bottle of claret and two glasses. Another elderly waiter creaked in under the weight of coffee-pot, milk and sugar on a heavy silver tray. Everything was placed on the coffee-table in front of the fire. A waiter opened the bottle of wine. 'We'll let it breathe for a moment. You lot go ahead with your coffee,' said the colonel.

Jennifer poured. Mary sat silently, twisting a handkerchief in her fingers. 'Are you feeling better, Mary?' asked Agatha.

'Oh, much better,' she said in a weak voice. 'But I had such a shock. I thought it was the ghost of Francie.'

'I didn't set out to make it look like anyone,' protested Harry. 'Just made a woman. Let's have that wine.'

The colonel poured two glasses.

'Look!' Daisy jumped to her feet. She ran to the window. 'Oh, do come and look at this.'

With the exception of Agatha, the others rose and went to the window and crowded behind her, saying, 'Where? What?'

Agatha tipped a few drops from the bottle into the colonel's glass. Then she stoppered the bottle and put it in her handbag. She looked quickly at the window. Harry was looking at her. Agatha said, 'Anything there? What is it?'

'A sea-gull,' said Jennifer in disgust. 'Daisy thinks a sea-gull is a harbinger of sunshine.'

'It's only because I haven't seen any until now,' said Daisy. 'I mean, they haven't been flying in the snow.'

'Sensible bird,' said the colonel tolerantly as he returned to his chair. 'Let's get to that wine, Harry.'

'Let me try it first,' said Harry. 'I'm fussier than you.' He raised his glass and took a sip. He wrinkled his nose. 'Don't have it, Colonel. It's corked.'

'You sure?'

'Yes, and there's nothing worse for the liver than bad wine.' Harry pressed the bell on the wall for the waiter. 'Take this away and bring us a decent one,' he said when the waiter had arrived. 'It's corked.'

The waiter bowed and removed the bottle and glasses.

Agatha looked at Harry and he stared blandly back at her. Had he seen anything?

'While he's bringing us another one,' said Harry, getting to his feet again, 'let me see if there's anything in that games cupboard to amuse us.' He rummaged in the cupboard and then shouted over his shoulder, 'There's Monopoly here. Fancy a game?'

'Haven't played that in ages,' said Jennifer. 'Bring it over.'

They all began to play Monopoly. The colonel and Harry drank steadily and then ordered another bottle.

The colonel became tipsy and began to flirt with Mary. Daisy was red with anger but Mary seemed to enjoy the flirtation and was giggling with delight.

At last, after a lengthy game, the colonel rose and stretched. 'Gottoliedown,' he said, making his sentence one slurred word. 'Whassat?' He pointed at the window.

'It's a snow-plough,' said Agatha, 'and the snow's stopped at last.'

With that, the lights suddenly came on. 'Great,' said Agatha. 'Let's hope the phones are on as well.'

She checked at reception and was told that, yes, the phones were back on. She went up to her room. The whole hotel was filled with creaks and groans as the elderly central heating system cranked into life.

Agatha phoned the police station but was told that Inspector Jessop was out. She hesitated then, wanting to phone Carsely to learn how James had reacted to the news of her engagement, but at the same time not wanting to, for fear of learning that there had been no reaction at all.

She decided to wait a little, had a bath, changed and went down for dinner. After she had eaten the first course, she realized the colonel had not put in an appearance.

'Where's Colonel Lyche?' she asked.

'Probably sleeping it off,' said Harry.

'You look all right,' said Daisy. 'I'm worried.'

Harry got to his feet. 'Well, dear lady, I will put your mind at rest.'

Daisy walked over to Agatha's table. 'He didn't drink it, did he?'

'The potion? Not even a sip.'

Daisy went back to her table.

After ten minutes, when Harry hadn't appeared, Agatha began to fret. God forbid anything had happened to the colonel.

Daisy threw down her napkin. 'I can't bear the waiting. I feel there's something wrong.'

'He used to drink like that,' said Mary soothingly. 'He'll be all right.'

But Daisy was already hurrying out.

Agatha picked at her main course, her appetite suddenly gone. Surely nothing had gone wrong. But if it had and if Harry had seen her put that potion in the colonel's glass . . .

A high penetrating scream sounded through the hotel. Agatha carefully put down her knife and fork. Jennifer jumped to her feet, knocking her chair over. She ran from the room, followed by Mary. Agatha stayed where she was, paralysed with dread. The orange lights of a gritter flashed outside the dining-room windows.

At last Agatha rose to her feet, feeling like an old woman. She went out into the hall.

It was empty. No one at the desk, no waiter around.

The silence seemed absolute.

Then an ambulance arrived, followed by two police cars. At the same time, Mr Martin hurried down the stairs, his face creased up with worry and distress. 'Upstairs,' he said to the ambulance men when they came in. They darted for the stairs, carrying a stretcher.

The police followed. No Jimmy.

Agatha stood rooted to the ground.

After what seemed an interminable age, the ambulance men reappeared carrying a stretcher. The figure on it was totally covered, the face hidden. Behind came Daisy, Jennifer, Mary and Harry. Daisy was being supported by Harry. Behind came the police, with Detective Sergeant Peter Carroll in the lead. At the foot of the stairs, Daisy broke away from Harry.

'Murderess!' she screamed at Agatha. Then she burst into noisy weeping.

And that was when the real nightmare for Agatha began.

That night, Agatha sat on a hard bunk in a cell in Wyckhadden police station and bleakly went over the events of the evening.

Harry Berry had told the police that out of the corner of his eye, when he had joined the others at the window after the colonel had ordered a bottle of claret, he thought he had seen Agatha slip something into the colonel's drink. He had not wanted to make a scene and he had not been sure of what he had seen and so he had decided to say the wine was corked and ask for another bottle. Daisy had told the police that Agatha had insisted on putting drops of a love potion into the colonel's drink. Agatha, Daisy had said, had been romancing the colonel and was jealous of her, Daisy. Therefore Agatha was a poisoner.

Agatha, at first sure that the love potion which had been taken from her handbag, along with every other bottle and jar in her room, was harmless, was beginning to worry. What if the murderer of Francie and Janine had wanted to be rid of the colonel and had doctored that love potion? What if it turned out to contain poison?

Jimmy had not come near her. He had not interviewed her, the superintendent from Hadderton had done that, a cold, hard man with suspicious eyes. Agatha had not been charged but was being kept in for further questioning. She had at last demanded a lawyer. He would be with her in the morning.

Rain pattered at the barred window above her head. God get me out of this, she prayed, and I will return to Carsely and never, ever leave it again.

* * *

As she did not know the names of any lawyers in the town, one had been supplied for her and he arrived in the morning. He listened carefully while Agatha outlined what had really happened. He was a middle-aged, tired-looking man with a thin face and gold-rimmed glasses and wearing a shabby suit.

'If that's your story, I would stick to it,' he said, when Agatha had finished. 'They'll need to charge you this morning or release you. The pathologist has been working all night on the body. These things take time.'

'Don't you believe me . . .' Agatha was starting to say impatiently when the cell door opened and Jimmy came in. He jerked his head at the lawyer and said, 'Leave us.'

'I cannot do that, Inspector,' said the lawyer. 'I am representing Mrs Raisin.'

'It's all right,' said Agatha. 'Leave us.'

When they were alone, Jimmy said, 'I'm sorry about this. I feel the police over-reacted.' He sat down on the bed next to Agatha and held her hand.

'I look a wreck,' said Agatha. 'They took my handbag away and I've no make-up on. What do you mean, they over-reacted?'

'I would say from a look at the colonel that he died of a massive stroke. His face had all slumped down to one side. I think that will turn out to be the case. What on earth were you doing messing with love potions, Agatha?'

'I went to Francie for that hair tonic. She offered that love potion as well and it seemed a bit of a joke at the time. Daisy was going frantic about the colonel. She had seen us at the theatre together and oh, I suppose I wanted to prove to her that I wasn't a bit interested in him. So I told her about the love potion.'

'There was only half a bottle left,' said Jimmy curiously.

'I started to pour it down the sink and then I thought it might be interesting to keep some and get it analysed when I got home,' said Agatha, who had no intention of telling Jimmy she had put some in *his* drink. 'What happens now?'

'They're more or less convinced, Agatha, that Colonel Lyche died of natural causes. You're free to go.'

'Jimmy, I not only want to go but I want to go back to Carsely.'

'I'm afraid that's not possible, Agatha. You'll need to wait for the definite result of the post-mortem, but it shouldn't be too long.'

'How do you put up with me, Jimmy?'

'Because I love you.'

Agatha felt a stab of guilt. What right had she to marry someone she didn't love? I do love him, she told herself fiercely, I'm just not *in* love with him.

'I'll have to keep clear of you until the final results of the post-mortem come through,' said Jimmy.

'I understand.' Again that stab of guilt because of the feeling of relief she had first felt at his words.

'I'll send a policewoman in to take you through to the desk to collect your things.'

'See you,' said Agatha wearily.

Agatha emerged from the police station into a watery world. Snow was sliding from roofs to fall with thuds on the street, water ran down the gutters and a mild, frisky wind blew through her hair.

She had hardly slept at all. She had refused the offer of a police car to take her back to the hotel. She opened her handbag and took out her packet of cigarettes, and turning her back to the wind, lit one. A thin, acidulous woman who was passing shouted at her, 'Don't you know that's a filthy habit?'

'Naff off!' shouted Agatha with such venom that the woman scurried off down the street.

Why did I ever come to this place? thought Agatha, as she trudged along the promenade beside the restless sea. At the end of the prom, she could see the hotel. It looked like a prison. What were they all doing? Playing Scrabble and talking about the weather?

Tired as she was, before she got to the hotel she turned and walked along the pier. There was a fascination in piers, those Victorian additions to the British coastline whose elegant spindly structures led out over the waves with their theatre or dance hall at the end, with their souvenir booths and slot machines. Her heels clacked on the boards. Someone had shovelled a clear pathway through the rapidly melting snow. She longed to be able to go up to her room and pack and get in that rented car and drive as far away as possible. She stood at the end of the pier looking down at the surging waves racing each other toward the shore until she began to shiver.

Wearily, she turned and walked towards the hotel. Mr Martin was at the desk.

'No calls,' snapped Agatha and went up to her room. Scrabble purred and mewed while Agatha prepared cat food and a bowl of water. She wanted a hot bath but she was so very tired. After Scrabble had been fed, Agatha climbed into bed without undressing, pulled the duvet up to her ears and plunged down into a dreamless sleep.

The Red Lion in Carsely was busy that lunchtime. Publican John Fletcher pulled a pint of Hook Norton for James Lacey and said, 'Our Agatha's in another mess.'

'What? There was nothing in the papers this morning,' said James.

'Heard it on the radio an hour ago,' said John. 'Some colonel died at that hotel Agatha's staying in. Agatha's been pulled in. Helping police with their inquiries, it said. You should go down there and see if you can help.'

'Her fiancé will look after her. He's a police inspector,' said James grimly and moved away from the bar.

Sir Charles Fraith was driving back to his estate when he heard the news about Agatha on the radio. 'Silly woman,' he muttered. When he got home, he phoned the Garden Hotel but was told that Mrs Raisin was not taking any calls.

What on earth was going on down there? he wondered. Might be fun to find out. Life had been a bit boring recently and the girl he had thought had fancied him like mad had just got engaged to someone else. He packed an overnight bag, got back in his car and headed south.

Agatha did not awake until evening. She soaked herself in a hot bath, washed her hair, then put on a night-dress and dressing-gown and phoned down to the desk and asked for sandwiches and coffee to be sent up. She did not feel like facing the others. She wanted to pretend they didn't even exist. The night porter had just come on duty. 'I have a note here to say you don't want any calls to be put through.'

'That's right,' said Agatha.

She switched on the television, which was showing an old James Bond movie. When her sandwiches arrived, Agatha settled down in a chair in front of the television with the cat on her lap to watch it.

Charles strolled into the Garden Hotel at nine that evening. The desk was empty. He peered into the lounge. It was empty apart from a tortoise-looking old man.

'Do you know where I can find Mrs Raisin?' he asked.

'I think she's in her room,' said Harry.

'Which one's that?'

'Number nine. Top of the stairs and turn left.'

Carrying his bag, Charles tripped up the stairs and turned left. There was a mirror in the corridor. He stopped and brushed down his smooth fair hair and studied his neat features. Then he went along and knocked on the door of number 9. No one answered but he could hear television noises. He tried the handle. Locked.

'Aggie! It's me!' he shouted. A dyed blonde woman with a blotchy face passed him in the corridor. Charles grinned at her. 'She must be deaf,' he said. He knocked again. 'Come on, Aggie. It's me, Charles!'

Agatha opened the door. 'Oh, Charles,' she said, 'I've been having such an awful time.'

And she burst into tears. He took her in his arms.

'It's all right. I'm here.'

Charles saw the blotchy-faced old blonde was watching them and propelled the weeping Agatha into the room and kicked the door shut behind him with his foot.

'What mess have you been getting yourself into?' He stroked her hair. 'Real hair, too.'

'It-it g-grew back,' sobbed Agatha into his shoulder.

'You're wetting my jacket. Any drink in this place?'

'Phone down for something.'

Charles picked up the phone and ordered a bottle of brandy. 'Which room?' asked the suspicious voice of the night porter.

'Mrs Raisin's room.'

'On her bill, sir?'

'Of course,' said Charles cheerfully.

He sat down on the bed. 'Now, come here and tell Charles all about it.'

Agatha dried her eyes and sat beside him. She told him everything from the beginning, only breaking off to answer the door and take in a tray with a bottle of brandy and two glasses.

'This is good of you, Charles.'

'Actually, it's on your bill.'

'You never change,' said Agatha. 'Here's thanks to me.' She continued her story while the brandy sank lower in the bottle.

'What a peculiar set-up,' said Charles. He lay back on the bed and clasped his hands behind his head.

'If you're staying the night,' said Agatha, 'then you'd best go and get yourself a room.'

'I've got a room,' said Charles lazily. 'Let's go to bed.'

'I don't like casual sex, Charles.'

'Who said it was casual?'

'You've proved in the past that it was casual.'

'Then let's just cuddle up.'

Agatha felt tipsy and tired and suddenly reluctant to be left alone.

'All right,' she said. But vanity made her go into the bathroom and put on some light make-up. When she returned, Charles had put on his pyjamas and was lying tucked up in bed, fast asleep.

So much for romance, thought Agatha, getting in beside him. Scrabble, curled on a chair, watched her curiously. The bedside light on Charles's side of the bed was burning. She leaned across him to put it out but before she could, his eyes opened and he smiled at her and wrapped his arms around her.

'None of that,' said Agatha, trying to pull free. He kissed her and then said mischievously, 'None of what? None of this?' He kissed her again. Janine's prediction that Agatha would never have sex again suddenly rang in her ears.

She told herself later that it was only to prove Janine wrong that she did.

Inspector Jimmy Jessop drove to the Garden Hotel. The results of the autopsy had come through. The colonel had died of natural causes. It was nearly midnight but he knew Agatha would thank him for letting her know as soon as possible. He wanted to tell her in person, to see the relief in her eyes.

He parked outside the Garden and walked in. Daisy came up to meet him, her face still swollen with crying and her eyes glittering oddly. Behind the desk, the night porter snored gently.

'Going to see Agatha?' asked Daisy.

'Yes.'

'Just go up,' said Daisy. 'Her room's number nine.'

Jimmy hesitated and looked towards the desk. 'I should phone first.'

'She's not receiving calls.'

'Oh, in that case . . .'

Jimmy headed for the stairs. Daisy gave a little smile and went back into the lounge.

Jimmy knocked softly at Agatha's door. There was no reply. He tried the handle. The door was unlocked. He opened it quietly.

The tableau that met his eyes was illuminated by a bedside lamp. There was a pair of man's striped pyjamas lying crumpled on the floor and Agatha's night-dress was hanging off the end of the bed.

Agatha herself was naked and wrapped in the arms of a man Jimmy did not know.

He retreated ever so quietly, closing the door with great care. He walked stiffly down the stairs and shook the night porter awake and demanded writing paper and an envelope.

Then he sat down and wrote Agatha Raisin a blistering letter, telling her exactly what he thought of her. A certain fairness prompted him to also tell her that the colonel had died of natural causes. She was therefore free to leave Wyckhadden and he never wanted to see her face again. He asked for his ring back. He sealed the letter and told the night porter to take it up and slide it under her door.

Agatha was the first to awake the following morning. She twisted round and looked at Charles's sleeping face, her first weary thought, Oh God, I've done it again. She pulled her night-gown up from the end of the bed and slipped it on. It was then she saw the envelope. She picked it up and sat down on the end of the bed and opened it.

She turned brick-red with shame and mortification. She threw the letter down and pulled off the engagement ring and put it on the bed-side table. Jimmy's letter made it perfectly clear that he had seen her in bed with Charles.

There was no way she could lie herself out of this one. And yet, at the root of all her shame was a little feeling of relief.

She prodded Charles in the ribs. 'Wake up!'

Charles struggled awake. 'What's the rush, dearest? I drove through this dismal little town last night, you know. Not the sort of place you leap out of bed for and with a glad cry go to explore.'

'Shut up and listen,' growled Agatha. 'Jimmy walked in last night and found us in bed together. He's broken off the engagement. He wants his ring back.'

'Let me see it.'

Agatha handed him the ring. He held it up to the light, squinted at it, and handed it back. 'Let him have it. Not worth keeping.'

'It's all your fault,' howled Agatha, goaded by his indifference.

'Show me the letter. Come on. You never even loved him, so don't pretend.'

Agatha gave him the letter. He read it carefully. 'Sounds like a good straight decent man. Not for the likes of you, Aggie.'

'How dare you!'

'And you're off the hook. You can come back with me.'

'Charles, do you not feel any remorse?'

'No, not a tittle, and neither would you if you hadn't been caught out.' He rose and strolled into the bathroom and closed the door.

Agatha reached for the phone to call Jimmy and then decided against it. What could she say? How could she explain herself? To say that she felt nothing for Charles would make her seem even more of a slut.

The phone rang. She picked it up gingerly as if it might bite and said a cautious 'Yes?'

'This is Mr Martin, Mrs Raisin.'

'How can I help you?'

'I believe you have a man in your room.'

'So what?' said Agatha crossly. 'This is the nineties.'

'It was booked as single accommodation. I must charge you double.'

'Go ahead, and get my bill ready. I'm leaving today,' snapped Agatha and replaced the phone.

She looked in the mirror and let out a squawk of alarm. He hair was all tousled and her unmade-up face looked old. Charles was at least ten years younger than she was. Then she sat down wearily. What did it matter? She wasn't in love with Charles. When he came out of the bathroom, she took his place and ran a bath and then found to her fury that he had used all the towels. She rang for fresh towels. No doubt those would go on her bill as well.

Charles, unconcerned and deaf to her complaints, was watching a morning television show.

Agatha finally bathed and changed and made up her face. Then she fed the cat and switched off the television in the middle of a game show. 'Now I'll never know who won the car,' complained Charles.

'We'll have some breakfast,' said Agatha, 'then I'll return my own car and buy a travelling cat box for Scrabble and you can run me to Carsely. I'd better drop in at the police station and return the ring.' She sat down at the desk. She would need to write to Jimmy.

'Okay,' said Charles indolently.

'By the way, how was it you just walked up to my room? Why didn't the desk phone me?'

'There was no one at the desk and when I looked into the lounge, there was a tortoise-looking old man who told me to go right up.'

'Harry,' said Agatha bitterly.

'I think he's mad, Agatha. In fact, they're probably all mad in this hotel. Did that ever occur to you? All of them sitting here, year in, year out, their old brains fossilizing?'

'Murder makes everyone seem mad,' said Agatha wearily, 'including me.' She wrote a brief note of apology to Jimmy, and put the ring in its little box. Then she stood up. 'Let's go. We'll eat later.'

Agatha, followed by Charles, drove to the car rental firm and turned in the car. Then she got in beside Charles and directed him to the police station.

'Want me to come in with you?' asked Charles.

'No, I won't be a moment.'

Agatha went into the police station. The police sergeant at the desk was talking to policewoman Trul and Detective Constable Tarret. They watched her in silence as she approached the desk.

Agatha handed the letter and jeweller's box over to the sergeant. 'Would you be so very good as to give this to Inspector Jessop?'

He silently took the box and letter. Agatha turned and walked out. 'Bitch!' said Trul loudly to her retreating back.

Her face flaming, Agatha got into the car beside Charles. 'It was awful,' she said. 'Jimmy must have told everybody.'

'What do you expect, you harlot?' laughed Charles. 'Where to?'

'I'll direct you to the car park in the centre of the town. I've got to buy a cat box.'

After she had purchased a cat box and Charles was driving sedately back to the hotel, he suddenly let out an exclamation and braked. 'Look at that!'

'What?'

'*Casablanca*'s showing at the cinema.'

'So?'

'I adore *Casablanca*. I want to see it. Showing at two this afternoon.'

'We're checking out at twelve.'

'One more night. I'll pay. Come on, Aggie.'

'Oh, all right. But you go on your own. I can't bear to see that old movie again.'

'And I'm starving. You didn't let us stop for breakfast.'

Mr Martin agreed that, yes, she could have the room for another night. 'He's paying,' said Agatha, jerking a thumb at Charles. 'We'll have lunch.'

They put their coats and the cat box up in the room and then went down to the dining-room. Jennifer, Mary, Daisy and Harry stared openly at them.

'What a bunch of freaks,' said Charles cheerfully. 'Very *Arsenic and Old Lace*.'

They ate their heavy lunch in silence. Then Charles went up to fetch his coat and go to the cinema. After he had left, Agatha began to feel the silence of the hotel oppressive. She wished she had not agreed to stay another night. What if Jimmy called and made a scene?

She realized the heavy meal and her activities of the night before had made her feel tired. Agatha lay down on the bed next to Scrabble and soon was fast asleep. She did not awake until six o'clock. She struggled up. Where was Charles?

James Lacey walked into the Garden Hotel. The television news had reported on the death of the colonel and said that Mrs Raisin was helping police with their inquiries, but there had been nothing further in that morning's news bulletin. He felt it was his duty for old times' sake to go down and see if he could help Agatha.

He was approaching the desk when the slim neat figure of Sir Charles Fraith walked past him.

'Charles!' called James.

'Hello,' said Charles cautiously.

'I came to see if I could help Agatha.'

'She's all right,' said Charles. 'That old boy died of natural causes. I'm just visiting.'

Suddenly Mr Martin was next to them. He said to Charles, 'As you are paying for the room you are sharing with Mrs Raisin, I would like you to sign the registration form.'

'What? Oh, sure,' said Charles, wilting before the blazing rage in James's eyes.

James turned on his heel and walked straight out of the hotel.

Charles miserably signed the registration form. Then he decided to go out and get a drink somewhere. If Agatha heard that her precious James had arrived and found out that they were sharing a room, she would be in a terrible rage.

Agatha had unpacked a few clothes. There was a knock at the door. 'Come in,' she called.

The door opened and Daisy walked in, staring round her curiously.

There was a hissing sound from the bed. Agatha turned and looked at Scrabble. The cat's eyes were blazing and its fur was standing on end.

Agatha looked at Daisy in a sort of wonder.

'It was you, wasn't it?' she said. 'It was you all the time.'

Chapter Nine

'That's Francie's cat,' said Daisy. 'What are you doing with Francie's cat?'

Agatha, hearing the odd crooning sound in Daisy's voice and looking at the vacant expression on her face, thought suddenly, she's mad. She's been mad all along, and none of us even noticed. But she said calmly, frightened that any loud sound or movement would tip Daisy over the edge, 'I found it wandering on the beach.' Scrabble was still hissing and spitting, green eyes ablaze.

'Sit down, Daisy. We have to talk.'

Daisy sat down. Agatha picked up Scrabble and shut the cat in the bathroom. 'The cat's seen you before. Come on. Out with it, Daisy.'

'Out with what?' She moved her head from side to side.

'Francie was blackmailing you.'

'It wasn't that,' said Daisy in a voice of mad reason. 'It wasn't that at all. She took my money.'

Agatha sat down on the bed. She wondered

why she felt so calm. 'There's just the two of us, Daisy. No police. Tell me about it.'

'It all happened so long ago,' said Daisy on a sigh. 'You won't tell anyone?'

'No,' said Agatha, thinking bleakly as she had no witnesses and no proof there was nothing she could do about it. The door was a little ajar. She thought of rising and closing it, but did not want to do anything to stop Daisy telling her story.

'My husband had died. I felt guilty. I suppose someone always feels guilty when someone dies.' She let out a girlish giggle, more horrible to Agatha's ears than if Daisy had ranted and raved. 'We had just had a terrible row, you see, and I felt it was my fault. He accused me of being in love with the colonel.'

'And were you . . . at that time?'

'Yes, I was very much in love with him. I was so relieved when Hugh died, but I thought God would punish me. I went to Francie to get in touch with Hugh, to find out if he was all right. Somehow Francie must have known something about my feelings for the colonel, seen the way I looked at him. It sounded like Hugh's voice. He said I had never loved him and I must pay. I think my brain was turned with guilt and fright. I gave Francie five thousand pounds.'

'What for?'

'She said she would pass it on to the spirit world. Then Harry told me she was a fake. I asked for my money back and she wouldn't give it to me.'

'Why didn't you report it to the police?'

'And look like a crazy old fool? I didn't think there was anything I could do. Then Harry let fall that maybe we could report Francie to the tax collector. He said when he had paid her, he had peeked into the other room and had seen her put the money in a cash box. I had sent people to Francie for potions. I discovered a lot about her and her habits, and I found out she had a nap late in the afternoon. I decided try to get at least some money back.

'I went along. The door was unlocked. She never locked it until the evening. I went quietly in. It was all so easy. I found the cash box. It wasn't even locked. I took out all the money. There was only about twelve hundred pounds in it. I stuffed it in my handbag.

'Then I decided to go upstairs and tell her what I had done. I knew as she probably hadn't declared any of the money to the taxman that she couldn't do anything about it. I thought she might try to attack me. I went into the kitchen looking for a weapon and saw a marble rolling pin. So useful, marble rolling pins.' She giggled again, and then put her hand up to her mouth and threw Agatha a coy, almost flirtatious look, like some schoolgirl confessing a misdemeanour to a headmistress.

'I crept up the stairs. She was lying sleeping. She suddenly opened her eyes and saw me.

"Oh, it's you, you silly old bitch," she said, and she reached down to the floor for her slippers. She shouldn't have called me old. One minute I was standing there with the rolling pin, and the next I had whacked her as hard as I could on the head.

'I didn't know if she was dead or not and I didn't care. I went out carrying the cash box and the rolling pin in a carrier bag. I threw the cash box in the sea. It was amazing. There was no one about. You see, I didn't care then if I was caught or not. But once I got rid of the cash box, I took the rolling pin back to the hotel. I had left by the fire escape. I buried the rolling pin in the hotel garden.'

Got you, thought Agatha.

'And what about Janine?'

'When it appeared that the murderer was going to be exposed, I kicked Mary as hard as I could. That broke up the seance. But I began to fret and worry. What if Janine knew? I thought the colonel was warming to me. I felt it would only be a matter of time before he proposed.' Daisy leaned forward and tapped Agatha on the knee. 'I had to get rid of her. You do see that?'

And Agatha remembered Charles saying that they were all probably mad. She *is* mad, thought Agatha again. Why didn't I see that before?

'So I went down the fire escape and I phoned her from that call box at the entrance to the pier. I wore gloves this time. I told her I owed her mother money and I would like her to have it but she wasn't to tell anyone.

'We walked along the pier. I said I had owed Francie thousands. Janine became quite excited. She was very like her mother, greedy. When we had gone along the pier a little way, I suddenly screamed and said, "There's a body floating in the water!" She said, "Where?" "Down there," I shouted. She leaned right over. I don't know where I got the strength but I seized her ankles and tipped her into the sea. She couldn't swim. Francie told me that once. She told me that neither she nor her daughter could swim. I heard her calling out, so I ran away.'

'Don't you feel any remorse?' asked Agatha curiously.

'Why?' Daisy's eyes glittered. 'They were bad women.'

'Couldn't you just have taken Francie's money and left it at that?'

'No! She cursed me, and Janine cursed me along with the rest of you. They were evil women.'

'Daisy, I am honour bound to go to the police and tell them what I've heard.'

'They won't believe you. You've no proof.'

And I'm not going to remind you that you told me about the rolling pin in the garden, Agatha was just thinking when Mr Martin walked in.

'I came up to talk to you, Mrs Raisin, but I

heard what was being said and I stayed to hear all of it. Mrs Daisy Jones, I am going to take you to your room and lock you in until the police arrive. Come along.'

To Agatha's amazement, Daisy stood up and smoothed down her skirt and walked out past the hotel manager. Why had she gone so quietly?

Charles walked in and Agatha flew to him, her nerves suddenly shot, babbling all about Daisy and the murders.

'Here, calm down, Aggie,' he said. 'Let's have it all – slowly.'

Agatha shakily summarized briefly what Daisy had told her, ending with, 'I cannot believe she went like that, so quietly.'

'Let's hope she doesn't remember telling you about that rolling pin.'

'Why?'

'Well, if she can find a way out of her room and down into the hotel garden, she'll do it.'

'The window!' gasped Agatha. 'The window in her room.' She hurtled out of the door and down the stairs and round to the side of the building. No Daisy in the garden.

'Up there!' cried Charles, suddenly appearing behind her.

Daisy was balancing on the ledge outside her window. Although her room was only one floor up, the downstairs ceilings were so high that she was a good distance from the ground.

She glared down at them. In the distance came the wail of police sirens.

'It's too late now,' shouted Agatha. 'Go back in your room. You'll only hurt yourself.'

But Daisy leaped from the window-ledge. She plummeted straight down on to a rockery. Her head struck one of the rocks with a vicious thud and she lay still.

Charles went up to her and bent down and stooped over her. 'I daren't move her,' he said over his shoulder to Agatha.

Agatha ran to the front of the hotel just as Jimmy Jessop was getting out of the first police car.

'It's Daisy,' said Agatha. 'She's in the garden. She's badly hurt.'

'Phone for an ambulance,' said Jimmy to a policeman. 'Lead the way, Mrs Raisin.'

The police followed Agatha into the hotel garden. Jimmy motioned Charles aside and knelt down beside Daisy. He felt for her pulse.

He looked up at them. 'I think it's too late. Go back into the hotel, Mrs Raisin, and you, too, sir. You will need to answer questions.'

Agatha felt sick and shaky. Supported by Charles, she went back into the hotel, to be met by Mary, Jennifer and Harry.

'Mr Martin's saying it was Daisy who committed these murders,' said Harry.

'It can't be true,' wailed Mary, and despite her dizziness and sickness, Agatha registered somewhere in her mind that neither Jennifer nor Harry seemed to be surprised.

Agatha said to Mr Martin, 'Tell the police I'll be in my room if they want me.'

She and Charles went upstairs. In their room, they both sat down on the bed. There was a plaintive mew from the bathroom. Agatha rose and let the cat out. Then she rejoined Charles.

'I don't know why you're so miserable, Aggie,' said Charles, taking her hand. 'If it hadn't been for your intuition and Scrabble's behaviour, she would have got away with it. And can I tell you something? You were probably next in line for the chop. I think Daisy's obsession with the colonel, which had been going on for years and years, had turned her mind. Sooner or later she would feel that he might have lived, might have married her if you hadn't lured him away.'

Agatha shivered. 'All I do is blunder about in other people's lives. When I get back to Carsely, I'm going to settle down and do good works.'

'That'll be the day,' said Charles with a laugh.

'I mean it. I'm going to be like Mrs Bloxby.'

Agatha rose. 'I'd better feed Scrabble. Any minute now they're going to come for us.'

'I'll do it.' Charles opened a can of cat food and then filled Scrabble's water bowl. 'Never mind, Aggie, we'll be out of here in the morning.'

There was a knock at the door. Charles answered it. A policeman stood there. 'If you would both accompany me to the police station . . .'

They collected their coats and followed him downstairs. 'Only one more night, please God,' said Agatha, looking out at the sea. 'Just one more night and then I will never come here again.'

At the police station, Agatha was interviewed by Jimmy and Detective Sergeant Peter Carroll.

She wearily began at the beginning and told them how Daisy had come to her room, the reaction of the cat, and how she'd suddenly known that Daisy had committed the murders.

'How did you know?' asked Carroll.

'I don't know,' said Agatha wretchedly. 'It was something Charles said about them all being mad. He was joking. But in that moment, I realized that Daisy was unbalanced.'

'In your statement about Mrs Frances Juddle's death,' said Carroll, 'you said her cat flew at you. So why should you think that Daisy was the murderess?'

'Just intuition,' said Agatha miserably. 'Will she live?'

'She's dead,' said Jimmy.

Agatha put her hands up to her face. 'I forgot about the rolling pin. That's why she was desperate to get down to the garden. She buried the rolling pin there.'

'Wait a minute.' They both left the room.

Agatha's knees were trembling. She put her hands on her knees.

After some time they came back. 'She didn't

say exactly where she had buried the rolling pin?' asked Carroll.

'Only that it was in the hotel garden,' said Agatha.

'We'll find it. Now let's go over it again. By the way, whatever cat you have in your room, it does not belong to the late Mrs Juddle.'

'What! Are you sure?'

'Cliff has the cat. We went to see him yesterday morning for another interview. He had the cat with him. So let's have it all from the beginning again.'

At last Agatha was free to go. 'I'll be leaving in the morning,' she said.

'I must ask you to be here for the coroner's inquest next week,' said Jimmy. 'You will be told of the time and place.'

'I'll never get out of here,' said Agatha bitterly.

'Leave us a minute,' said Jimmy to Carroll.

When they were alone, Jimmy said quietly, 'Sit down, Agatha.'

Agatha sat down, her eyes filling with tears.

'If it hadn't been for you, we might not have got her,' said Jimmy. 'The reason I want to speak to you is I have enough affection left for you to warn you.'

Agatha took a Kleenex out and dried her eyes. 'About what?'

'About Sir Charles.'

'What about him?' asked Agatha, turning pink.

'I assume that the fact he is a baronet and younger than you might have gone to your head, Agatha, but if you have any thoughts of becoming Lady Fraith, I would forget it.'

'I never thought for a moment –'

'Sir Charles said you were nothing more than casual friends who had an occasional fling. He said it meant nothing. I do not belong in your world, Agatha. I do not believe in casual sex.'

'Neither do I, Jimmy.'

'Then you are a sad case. It was definitely casual to him and he made no bones about it.'

Agatha stood up. 'I would like to leave.'

He nodded and she went out.

Charles was sitting waiting for hcr. 'I want a word with you,' said Agatha grimly. 'Let's walk.'

When they were outside the police station, Charles said with attempted cheerfulness, 'No press yet. But they'll be all over the placc soon.'

'Charles, was it necessary for you to make me feel even more like a tart by telling them I meant nothing to you?'

'I didn't exactly say that. Your inspector looked so low and I thought I had messed up your life. He's a really decent chap and you could do much worse. I was only trying to help.'

'Listen, you moron, such as Jimmy Jessop would never even look at a woman who went in for casual sex.'

'Doesn't he know it's the nineties?'

'Oh, *Charles*. You are a pig.'

He tucked her arm in his. 'Don't let's quarrel. How late is it? I suppose the dining-room at the hotel's closed. Oh, look, there's a fish-and-chip shop.'

They ate fish and chips on the road back to the hotel.

Then they went into the hotel.

'No, proper names are not allowed,' came Harry's voice from the lounge. 'You know that, Jennifer.'

'They're still playing Scrabble,' marvelled Agatha. 'People get murdered, people fall out of windows, and they still play Scrabble. Oh, by the way, would you believe it, I've got the wrong cat.'

'What?'

'Scrabble isn't Francie's cat.'

'Then maybe Daisy came to your room to do you wrong. Animals sense danger.'

Mr Martin approached them. 'This is terrible, terrible,' he said. 'We're ruined.'

'Oh, let the press in,' said Agatha wearily. 'They'll drink a lot and spend a lot. And when the Season starts, you'll have a full house. People are very ghoulish. Your hotel will be famous.'

'But our residents won't like the press here.'

'There's only the three of them left,' said

Charles. 'Why shouldn't you make some money out of all this tragedy? The press are big spenders. They'll drink your bar dry.'

Mr Martin brightened. 'I suppose they won't be here that long.'

'Exactly,' said Agatha.

She and Charles went upstairs.

'No funny business tonight,' said Agatha severely.

'You do have a way with words, Aggie,' said Charles.

But Agatha Raisin felt rather peeved when he finally got into bed and started to read one of her paperbacks and was still reading when she went to sleep.

By morning, before they left the hotel, there was a telephone call from the police telling them that the inquest would be on Wednesday at the coroner's court at ten in the morning.

'Cheer up, Aggie,' said Charles as they drove out of Wyckhadden, 'you'll only need to see the wretched place one more time.'

Agatha tried very hard on the road home to banish thoughts of James Lacey from her mind. But she imagined over and over again the pair of them sitting in some Cotswold restaurant while she told her story.

Finally Charles parked outside her cottage and helped her in with her suitcase and cat box.

'I won't stay, Aggie. I'll call round next Wednesday about six-thirty in the morning and pick you up for the inquest. Or, if you like, we could go down the night before.'

Agatha repressed a shudder. 'No, I don't mind an early start.'

When Charles had left, she let the cat out of its box. To her relief her other two cats, Boswell and Hodge, seemed to accept the newcomer. She fed them and turned them out into the garden.

Then she picked up the phone and called James Lacey. There was no reply, nor had his car been outside his house.

She walked along to the vicarage. 'Oh, good, you're back,' said Mrs Bloxby. She called to her husband, 'Agatha's back.'

The vicar rose and bolted out of the door. 'Going to the church,' he called.

'Come in,' said Mrs Bloxby, 'and sit down. It's all over the newspapers.'

'Do they say it was me who found out the murderess?' asked Agatha.

'No, they say something about the hotel manager having overheard Daisy Jones telling one of the residents she had done it. Was it you? How clever. Tell me about it.'

So Agatha told her story and as she talked in the quiet calm of the vicarage living-room, it all began to seem very strange and far away.

'And what about your inspector? You haven't mentioned him.'

'It's all off. He found me in bed with Charles.'

'How awful. But you are not heart-broken.'

'Just very ashamed. Jimmy's a good man. I regret losing him. I could have made it work.'

'But you don't love him, and if you married him, you would have to live in Wyckhadden.'

'God forbid. I've never known a place with such changes in weather. There'll probably be a tornado on the day of the inquest.'

'We had bad weather here. Terrible floods. The rescue boats were out in the streets of Evesham and even Moreton-in-Marsh was flooded.'

'So where's James?' asked Agatha abruptly.

'He left his key with Fred Griggs.' Fred Griggs was the village policeman. 'He told Fred he was going to stay with some people in Sussex.'

'So he'll be back soon?'

'It seems like that.'

So Agatha watched and waited, hoping always to see James Lacey's car drive up to his cottage.

James arrived home late on the evening before the inquest. He did his laundry and then packed his suitcase again. He had made arrangements to go to Greece. He thought briefly of calling on Agatha in the morning to say goodbye. But he didn't want to hear her burbling on about her inspector.

The sound of a car stopping outside Agatha's cottage early in the morning awoke him. He struggled out of bed and went to the side window on the half-landing and looked down at the entrance to Agatha's cottage. She emerged with Charles. They got in Charles's car. They looked very happy.

He went back to bed.

He was part of Agatha Raisin's past now, so he would make damn sure she stayed part of his.

The inquest was less harrowing than Agatha had imagined. She and Charles told their stories.

The press were waiting outside. But Agatha had been too subdued by the sight of Jimmy in the court to grab her moment of glory. She got in Charles's car, deaf to the questions and ignoring the flashes going off in her face.

'Goodbye forever,' she said as Charles drove out of the town.

Chapter Ten

Three months later, Agatha Raisin stood behind the tombola stand at a fund-raising venture for Save the Children. It was a worthy cause and she had worked hard on the organizing committee to make the fair a success. She felt her eyes should now look out on the world with the same quiet glow of serenity in them that she saw in Mrs Bloxby's eyes. She took out her compact and looked in the little mirror. A pair of bearlike eyes stared bleakly back at her.

James had gone to Greece and Agatha had to admit to herself that she was bored. 'I bought three tickets and all I got was a tin of sardines,' grumbled old Mrs Boggle.

'With tickets at twenty pee each, you got a bargain,' snapped Agatha.

'I know what it is,' said Mrs Boggle, 'you're keeping all the best prizes for yourself.' Agatha ignored her and sold more tickets. To her delight and under the envious eyes of Mrs Boggle, the next two people won, respectively, a bottle of whisky and a hamper of selected cheeses. Mrs Boggle bought another ticket. She won a bottle of shampoo. 'There you are,' said Agatha brightly. 'You can't complain about that.' But of course Mrs Boggle did, saying she had wanted the whisky. The day wore on. The jingly-jangly music of the morris dances began to get on Agatha's nerves.

She was restless and wanted some excitement. She had phoned Charles, but he had cheerfully said he was busy and Agatha knew that 'busy' with Charles meant he was in pursuit of some female.

On this sunny day, with bunting fluttering in the lightest of breezes, her thoughts turned again to Jimmy. Her cottage at night no longer seemed a sanctuary, a refuge, but lonely and boring, with only the television for company. Mrs Bloxby had tried to help the 'new' Agatha to sainthood by suggesting that their next move would be to help out at a charity fête in Longborough.

If I had married Jimmy, thought Agatha wistfully, I would be part of a pair, I would be Mrs Jessop. The police had returned the love potion and hair restorer. Agatha had sent them both to a lab in Birmingham for analysis. The love potion turned out to be aniseed-flavoured water and the hair restorer was a bottle of commercial stuff, available on the market for twenty-five pounds. All Francie had done was remove the label. But it meant that no magic had made Jimmy fall for her. He was not like James Lacey, bad-tempered and chilly, or Charles, fickle and amoral. He was a decent man and he had loved her and he had given her his ring.

Wyckhadden had been all right, thought Agatha, automatically selling tickets and smiling and handing out prizes. It was only the murders and the dreadful weather which had made it seem so awful.

And then she began to wonder if she could get Jimmy back. She could explain about Charles, explain that she had been upset and had drunk too much. He would give her that warm smile of his and she would feel secure. She began to forget that stab of relief she had experienced when she had known that the engagement was over.

Why not go back to Wyckhadden and just see if she could talk to him?

The idea of taking action, some action, any action, began to get a grip of Agatha.

She began to feel happy in a way that no amount of good works had managed to make her feel.

At the end of the day, she began to help clear up. Mrs Bloxby, looking with some surprise at Agatha's happy face, thought that perhaps Agatha really was meant for good works.

That was until Agatha told her she planned to go back to Wyckhadden and see Jimmy. Mrs Bloxby was about to protest that Agatha would probably only meet with rejection, Mrs Bloxby being more used to the Jimmy Jessops of this world – that is, ordinary decent people – than Agatha, but decided against it. Perhaps Jimmy might turn out to be the man for Agatha after all. She had only Agatha's word for it that he was an ordinary decent man. And the world was full of women who had married for companionship and security, so why not Agatha? So she fought down the voice of her conscience that was telling her that Agatha Raisin would be miserable with less, and wished her luck.

Agatha did not immediately dash off. She went to the beautician's and had a facial and her eyebrows shaped. Then the hairdresser's, then into a new boutique beside the hairdresser's in Evesham to choose something new. She hesitated between selecting something pretty and feminine or something sharp and businesslike. At last she bought a biscuit-coloured linen suit and a soft, pale yellow silk blouse to go with it. Then she drove back to Carsely and called round to see her cleaner, Doris Simpson, to tell her that she was going away again, but just for a few days, and that there was now an extra cat to feed.

Feeling more and more confident, she had a good night's sleep and set out on the long road to Wyckhadden early the following morning.

As she drove into Wyckhadden past neat little villas and bungalows on the outskirts, she looked at them with new eyes. She could live a life in one of those, mowing the lawn and polishing the car.

She drove straight to the Garden Hotel. The weather was warm on the beach and the kiosks on the pier were open. The sea, which had looked so threatening in the winter, was tamed into calm deep blue. A ship puffed along the line of the horizon, looking like a child's toy.

In the hotel, there was now a glamorous receptionist behind the desk and guests were coming and going.

The receptionist smiled and said Agatha was lucky. They had received a cancellation that morning. There was a smart young foreign porter in new hotel livery to carry her bag up to her room. The old hotel had an air of life and prosperity. Agatha wondered whether Harry, Jennifer and Mary were still in residence or if the big influx of new guests had driven them away. But then, they had said they were used to visitors.

Agatha picked up the phone and got through to the police station. 'Wyckhadden police,' came the voice of the desk sergeant. 'I would like to speak to Inspector Jessop,' said Agatha.

'Yes. May I ask who's calling?'

'Agatha Raisin.'

'He's out on a case,' said the desk sergeant sharply.

'When is he due back?'

'We don't know. Not for a long time.'

'I am staying at the Garden Hotel. Would you ask him to phone me?'

'If I see him,' said the desk sergeant ungraciously and replaced the receiver.

She changed into the new linen suit and blouse and walked down to the hall. She asked for Mr Martin.

Mr Martin came out of his office and looked at her like the Ancient Mariner spotting the albatross. 'Oh, dear . . . I mean, how nice to see you again.'

'I wondered if Miss Stobbs, Miss Dulsey and Mr Berry were still in residence.'

'Yes, they are.' He looked at the line of keys behind the desk. 'They all appear to be out at the moment. Er, will you be staying long?'

'A couple of days,' said Agatha.

Agatha went out into the sunshine and walked along the pier. She wished she had brought her coat, for although the sun was warm, the sea breeze was somewhat chilly. She then saw that among the souvenir kiosks, there was a new booth: MADAM MYSTIC, FORTUNE-TELLER.

May as well pass the time until I figure out what to do, thought Agatha.

Madam Mystic was dressed in a long black robe and wore a turban on her head.

'Sit down,' she said. 'Your fortune will cost you ten pounds.'

'Right.'

'Money now.'

Agatha paid over a ten-pound note.

'Let me see your hands,' said Madam Mystic.

Agatha held out her hands. 'You are a healthy, determined woman with a lot of success and money in her life, but not love.'

'And will I get any?' asked Agatha, wondering, why did I come to this charlatan?

'Perhaps, but you must go to look for it. You live in a small place where nothing happens.'

That's what you think, thought Agatha.

'The love of your life is in Norfolk. He is tall with fair hair. He is a widower. You must go in search of him.'

'Norfolk's a big county. Where? North, south, east or west?'

'You drive to Norfolk and something will guide you.'

She fell silent.

'Anything else?'

'You must not stay in Wyckhadden. Forget what brought you here and go home.'

'What? Not to Norfolk?'

'You will go there eventually. I cannot see any more.'

I must stop wasting money, Agatha chided herself. She walked out into the sunshine.

And there she saw Harry Berry, leaning on the rail of the pier watching some anglers.

Agatha went up to him. 'Hello, Harry.'

He turned round. 'Oh, it's you,' he said. 'What brings you back?'

'I was at a loose end. I thought I would look up Jimmy Jessop.'

Harry's eyes shone briefly with amusement.

'The hotel seems to be doing well,' said Agatha.

'It's not the same place. First, we were full of press, then ghouls wanting to see the room where Daisy fell from the window, then word got around about the meals being sumptuous, and all sorts of tourists started coming.'

'How are Jennifer and Mary?'

'Fine, but we're all thinking of moving somewhere quieter.'

'Was it a great shock to learn that Daisy was a murderess?'

Harry turned back and stared down at the water. 'Not really.'

'What! Never tell me you knew all along.'

'It was just a feeling,' said Harry. 'The colonel often said he thought it was Daisy.'

'What! I thought none of you ever talked about the murder.'

'Well, we did, when you weren't around.'

So much for feeling part of the group, thought Agatha bitterly. 'Why was I such an outsider that nothing was mentioned to me?'

'We thought you might make a fuss, and we don't like fuss.'

'So why didn't you go to the police?'

'Why? We could've been wrong and Daisy was one of us.'

Agatha looked at him. 'That snow-woman,' she said slowly. 'You tried to make it as much like Francie as possible in the hope that Daisy might betray herself.'

'Could have been something like that. It's over now, poor Daisy.'

'Poor Daisy. She murdered two women.'

'They were murderees. If it hadn't been Daisy it would have been someone else.'

'See you later.' Agatha turned and walked away. Charles had been right. They *were* mad.

She decided to go to that pub and see if Jimmy turned up. She was perfectly sure he had not been out on a case. The desk sergeant was simply trying to keep her away from him.

She waited in the pub for an hour but there was no sign of Jimmy. She went back to the hotel and got her car and drove to the police station and waited outside. Wyckhadden seemed to have returned to being a relatively crime-free zone. Hardly anyone came or went. The day wore on. She had made an early start and was beginning to feel sleepy.

Then she saw his tall figure emerging from the police station. She fumbled for the door handle of the car, wrenched open the door and called, 'Jimmy!'

He turned and saw her and that old familiar glad smile lit up his face. He still loves me, thought Agatha. Thank God. She hurried towards him.

'This is a surprise,' he said. 'What brings you back?'

'I felt so badly about the way I treated you. I wanted to see you again.'

'Let's go for a drink,' said Jimmy, tucking her arm in his. 'I've a lot to tell you.'

They walked to a nearby pub. How could I ever have disliked this town, thought Agatha happily. I'll live here with my Jimmy for the rest of my life.

'Your usual, Agatha?' Agatha nodded. It was like old times. Jimmy got her a gin and tonic and a half pint of lager for himself.

'Now tell me, what's happening?' asked Agatha. She caught a glimpse of herself in a mirror opposite: shining brown hair, well made up, neat linen suit, she felt secure and content.

Jimmy put his hand over hers and looked into her eyes.

'I'm getting married, Agatha, and it's thanks to you.'

Agatha stared at him. Then she looked at the mirror. A tired middle-aged woman looked back.

'It's like this,' said Jimmy eagerly. 'I was shocked rigid at your behaviour with that baronet. I thought I'd never look at another woman again. And then Gladwyn walked into the police station.

'Gladwyn Evans.' Jimmy flushed slightly

and removed his hand from Agatha's. 'She's a young widow. Only thirty-five. There had been a burglary at her home, and do you know what, she lives practically next door to me, but what with work and the murders, I hadn't had time to notice her. She'd only moved here recently. We got friendly. I found myself telling her all about you.'

Agatha groaned inwardly.

'She was most sympathetic and with her living so near, we began to see a lot of each other and then she began preparing meals for me. I couldn't believe that such a pretty young woman would want to look after me. I didn't dare make a move until she said, just like that, "Why don't we get married?" It was the talking about you that got us discussing all sorts of intimate things, you see.'

'I'm very happy for you,' said Agatha. 'What about . . . er . . . the other problem?'

'Impotence? Forget it.' He leaned back in his chair and laughed. 'Gladwyn's pregnant! And I'm a father-to-be. Me, at my age. I feel I've won the lottery. No, *better* than winning the lottery.'

'Here's to you,' said Agatha faintly, raising her glass.

'Let's go and meet her.'

'What?'

'You *would* like to meet her, wouldn't you?'

'Yes, that would be very nice,' said Agatha weakly. She wanted to run away, far away.

But she meekly left the pub with Jimmy and they walked back to their cars. 'I forget where you live, Jimmy.'

'Just follow me.'

So Agatha followed his car, although she longed to swing the wheel and head for the Garden, pack up and go home. Wyckhadden now seemed a hostile place, a place full of contemptuous eyes.

Gladwyn was young, yes, but she was probably some sort of housewifely frump with thick glasses and greasy hair. So Agatha consoled herself as she got out of her car and followed Jimmy up his garden path.

The door was opened by a plump, black-haired Welsh woman with smooth white skin and large brown eyes. 'You'll never guess who this is!' cried Jimmy. 'Agatha Raisin!'

A flash of shock followed by a flash of pure hatred flickered in Gladwyn's large eyes and then she smiled. 'Come in.'

Agatha went into Jimmy's transformed bungalow. The walls had been painted in warm pastel colours. There was a sewing machine set up in the living room, a cosy clutter of magazines and books and framed prints on the walls.

'I'll get tea,' said Gladwyn in a lilting voice, 'and leave you to talk.'

'You'll need to see the nursery before you go,' said Jimmy. 'Oh, there's something else. You know that fur coat of yours?'

'Yes.'

'Gladwyn knows this furrier and he did a beautiful job of restoring it. It looks like new. You don't mind?'

'No,' said Agatha who suddenly found she minded like hell.

'Did you find that rolling pin?' asked Agatha.

'Yes, it was indeed buried in the garden.'

'And I suppose from DNA samples you identified any traces of blood on it as Francie's?'

Jimmy snorted. 'Don't talk to me about DNA. Do you know there's a backlog of one hundred thousand cases? The police are having to drop cases because the evidence is not coming up in time for the court case. Good thing she killed herself. Saves the public purse all that money for a trial and for lengthy imprisonment. We'd never have suspected her. I kept feeling sure it was Janine's husband.'

'What happened about that business with the Ferris wheel?'

'Nothing or you might have been called back for some court case. They all stuck together and swore blind it was a faulty piece of mechanism. Isn't life odd, Agatha? If you'd come back here before I met Gladwyn, I would have hated you, would have had nothing to do with you. But now I'm really in love, it all seems like a miracle and all I can think is that it's because of you that these nasty murders got solved and because of you, I was able to talk to Gladwyn about my feelings and emotions.'

'You are a very forgiving man,' said Agatha, wondering whether she were as mad as Jennifer, Mary and Harry. How could she have possibly believed that she could just walk back into his life after the way she had treated him?

Gladwyn came in bearing a tea tray and a plate of home-made cakes.

'What brought you to Wyckhadden?' asked Agatha politely.

'It was about a year after the death of my husband,' said Gladwyn. 'I wanted to make a new start in a new place where there weren't any memories. I sold up in Merthyr Tydfil and moved down here. I've always liked the sea. Oh, did Jimmy tell you about the coat?'

'Yes, and I'm glad you're wearing it.'

'I'll show you.' Gladwyn went out and returned after a few moments with the mink coat wrapped round her. The furrier had done a beautiful job. Agatha felt a lump in her throat. She remembered the days when fur was fashionable, walking down Bond Street in that very coat, feeling like a million dollars, a younger, ambitious Agatha with the world at her feet, and no silly yearnings for love to clutter up her mind.

'It looks marvellous on you.'

'I can't take it on our honeymoon,' laughed Gladwyn.

'Where are you going?'

'Benidorm, Spain.'

'It'll certainly be hot.'

'Come and see the nursery,' said Gladwyn.

I must get out of here before I cry, thought Agatha desperately.

She followed Gladwyn through to a small bedroom. The walls were decorated with stencils of bluebirds and teddy bears. A new cot stood by the window and beside it a box full of fluffy toys.

'Gladwyn did all the painting and decoration herself,' said Jimmy. 'There's nothing she can't do.'

Agatha looked at her watch and let out a stagy exclamation of surprise. 'That time already! I must fly. I'm meeting someone.'

'I'll just go to the bathroom,' said Jimmy, 'and then I'll see you out.'

Agatha walked towards the door. She and Gladwyn stood on the step. Gladwyn turned to her and said in a low voice, 'If you ever come back here again, you old bitch, I'll strangle you. Leave my Jimmy alone. What he ever saw in an old frump like you, is beyond me.'

Jimmy came up and joined them. Agatha wanted to hurl insults at Gladwyn, but restrained herself.

She shook hands with Jimmy, nodded to Gladwyn, and on stiff legs walked down the garden path. She got into her car. They were standing side by side on the doorstep.

Agatha waved. Jimmy turned and went inside. Gladwyn gave Agatha a two fingered sign, turned and followed him.

Agatha drove around the corner, stopped the car and leaned against the wheel, breathing heavily. Why had she been such a fool? Face up to it, she told herself fiercely, Jimmy has been very, very lucky. You would have driven him mad within a week.

She released the hand brake, let in the clutch and drove slowly and carefully back to the Garden.

She went up to her room and took off the linen suit. It was unlucky. She would never wear it again. She changed into a dark red blouse and velvet skirt and went down for dinner. The hotel now boasted a maitre d' who told her that as the hotel was so busy, he had placed her at a table with two other ladies. The two other ladies turned out to be Jennifer and Mary.

'Why, Agatha,' said Jennifer, 'it *is* you. Are you staying down for Inspector Jessop's wedding?'

'You know about that?' Agatha shook out her napkin.

'Yes, Harry and Mary and me have all been invited.'

'Why?'

'Well, you see, he got a lot of kudos for solving those murders . . .'

'I solved them.'

'Anyway, he asked the three of us. Isn't it fun?'

So Harry knew all about the wedding, thought Agatha, and yet he said nothing. Does everyone want to hurt me?

'How's everything?' she said.

'We're really thinking of moving to Eastbourne. This hotel's not the same and Mr Martin has put the rates up.' Mary leaned forward. 'The food's not the same either. You'll see.'

Mary was proved right. The portions were considerably smaller.

'Martin's a fool,' said Agatha. 'Why is it that when places get popular, they stint on the food and raise the rates?'

'He's got a lot of new staff to pay,' said Mary. 'I say, we're going to a dance on the pier tonight. Want to come?'

'Why not?' said Agatha.

But when she went up to her room after dinner, she suddenly began thrusting all her clothes back into her suitcase. She carried it down to the desk and paid her bill. 'Family troubles,' she said to the surprised receptionist. 'Got to go.'

As she drove out of Wyckhadden, she repressed a superstitious shiver. Janine had cursed them all. Daisy and the colonel were dead. Which one next?

She drove along the promenade, now hung with fairy lights. And coming along arm in arm were Jimmy and Gladwyn. Gladwyn was wearing the mink coat. I hope some animal libber murders her, thought Agatha fiercely. Why can't I get away with being unpolitically correct? People even swear at me for smoking.

How weary and how lonely and how long the road back to Carsely seemed.

When she finally let herself into her cottage, she checked her answering service. No one had phoned, no Charles, no James, no one from the village.

She went wearily to bed surrounded by cats.

'So,' said Mrs Bloxby sympathetically the next day. 'It was a disaster.'

'Total humiliation,' said Agatha who had called to tell the vicar's wife all about it.

'It wouldn't have worked, you know,' said Mrs Bloxby. 'He wouldn't ever have trusted you and every time you had a marital quarrel, Charles's name would be thrown in your face. It's this craving for excitement that emanates from you. You'll always stir things up.'

'Not any more,' said Agatha. 'I'm weary. I'm settled. Me and my cats.'

'I hope so. There's a meeting of the ladies' society here tomorrow.'

'I'll come. I'll help you with the catering.'

'That is good of you.' Mrs Bloxby then prattled on about village affairs and the latest fund raising project. At last Agatha rose and took her leave.

'Has that awful woman gone?' asked the vicar, popping his head round the study door.

'You're very hard on her, Alf,' said Mrs Bloxby. 'She's got a good heart.'

The vicar kissed his wife on the top of her head and smiled down at her fondly. 'You love everyone.'

'And you forget that's supposed to be part of your job.'

'What does she think of James's blonde moving in?'

Mrs Bloxby looked uncomfortable. 'I hadn't the heart to tell her.'

'Coward!'

Agatha walked back to Lilac Lane where her cottage was. It was then she saw a long, low, red sports car parked outside James's cottage and smoke rising from the chimney.

He was home! All her misery fled. They would sit and talk and she would tell him all about the murders. She knocked on his door.

It was opened by a tall slim blonde, thirty-something, wearing cut-off jeans and one of James's shirts knotted at the waist.

'Is James at home?' asked Agatha.

'No, he's in Greece. I met him there. He said I could use the cottage until he got back.'

'When will that be?'

'Don't know. Isn't he a sweetie?'

'Yes. See you.'

Agatha clumped off to her own cottage. She fed the cats and let them out into the garden.

There was an aching pain where her heart should be.

If you enjoyed *The Witch of Wyckhadden*, read on for the first chapter of the next book in the *Agatha Raisin* series . . .

AGATHA RAISIN
and the
FAIRIES OF FRYFAM

Chapter One

Agatha Raisin was selling up and leaving Carsely for good.

Or rather, that had been the plan.

She had already rented a cottage in the village of Fryfam in Norfolk. She had rented blind. She knew neither the village nor anywhere else in Norfolk. A fortune-teller had told her that her destiny lay in Norfolk. Her next door neighbour, the love of her life, James Lacey, had departed without saying goodbye and so she had decided to move to Norfolk and had chosen the village of Fryfam by sticking a pin in the map. A call to the Fryfam police station had put her in touch with a local estate agent, the cottage was rented, and all Agatha had to do was sell her own cottage and leave.

But the problem lay in the people who came to view the house. Either the women were too attractive and Agatha was not going to have an attractive woman living next door to James, or they were sour and grumpy, and she did not want to inflict such people on the village.

She was due to move into her rented Norfolk cottage at the beginning of October and it was now heading to the end of September. Bright-coloured autumn leaves swirled about the Cotswold lanes. It was an Indian summer of lazy mellow sunny days and misty nights. Never had Carsely seemed more beautiful. But Agatha was determined to get rid of her obsession for James Lacey. Fryfam was probably beautiful as well.

Agatha was just stiffening up her weakening sinews when the doorbell rang. She opened the door. Two small round people stood there. 'Good morning,' said the woman brightly. 'We are Mr and Mrs Baxter-Semper. We've come to view the house.'

'You should have made an appointment with the estate agent,' grumped Agatha.

'Oh, but we saw the "For Sale" board outside.'

'Come in,' sighed Agatha. 'Take a look around. You'll find me in the kitchen if you have any questions.'

She hunched over a cup of black coffee at the kitchen table and lit a cigarette. Through the window, she could see her cats, Hodge and Boswell, playing in the garden. How nice to be a cat, thought Agatha bitterly. No hopeless love, no responsibility, no bills to pay, nothing else to do but wait to be fed and roll around in the sun.

She could hear the couple moving about. Then she heard the sound of drawers being opened and closed.

She went to the foot of the stairs and shouted up, 'You're supposed to be looking at the *house,* not poking among my knickers.' There was a shocked silence. Then they both came downstairs. 'We thought you might be leaving your furniture behind,' said the woman defensively.

'No, I'm putting it into storage,' said Agatha wearily. 'I'm renting in Norfolk until I find somewhere to buy.'

Mrs Baxter-Semper looked past her.

'Oh, is that the garden?'

'Obviously,' said Agatha, blowing smoke in her direction.

'Look, Bob. We could knock down that kitchen wall and have a nice conservatory.'

Oh, God, thought Agatha, one of those nasty white wood-and-glass excrescences sticking out of the back of *my* cottage.

They stood before her as if expecting her to offer them tea or coffee.

'I'll show you out,' said Agatha gruffly.

As she shut the door behind them with a bang, she could hear Mrs Baxter-Semper saying, 'What a rude woman!'

'House is perfect for us, though,' remarked the husband.

Agatha picked up the phone and dialled the estate agents. 'I've decided not to sell at the moment. Yes, this is Mrs Raisin. No, *I don't want to sell*. Just take your board down.'

When she replaced the receiver, she felt happier than she had done for some time. Nothing could be achieved by quitting Carsely.

'So you have decided not to go to Norfolk?' exclaimed Mrs Bloxby, the vicar's wife, later that day. 'I am so glad you aren't leaving us.'

'Oh, but I am going to Norfolk. May as well get a change for a bit. But I'll be back.'

The vicar's wife was a pleasant-looking woman with grey hair and mild eyes. In her ladylike clothes of flat shoes, droopy tweed skirt, silk blouse and ancient cardigan, she looked the exact opposite of Agatha Raisin, a stocky figure with excellent legs in sheer stockings and sporting a short tailored skirt and jacket. Her glossy hair was cut in a chic bob and her bearlike eyes, unlike those of Mrs Bloxby, looked out at the world with a defensive, wary suspicion.

Although they were close friends, they still often called each other by their second names – Mrs Bloxby, Mrs Raisin – as was the old-fashioned custom of the Carsely Ladies' Society to which they both belonged.

They were sitting in the vicarage garden. It was a late-autumn afternoon, mellow and golden.

'And what about James Lacey?' asked Mrs Bloxby gently.

'Oh, I've nearly forgotten about him.'

The vicar's wife looked at Agatha steadily. The day was quiet. One late rose bloomed in red glory against the mellow golden walls of the vicarage. Beyond the garden lay the churchyard, the sloping gravestones sending shadows across the tussocky grass. The clock in the church tower bonged out six o'clock.

'The nights are drawing in,' said Agatha. 'Well, no, I haven't got over James. That's the idea of going away. Out of sight, out of mind.'

'Doesn't work.' Mrs Bloxby tugged at a loose piece of wool on her cardigan. 'You're letting someone live rent-free in your head.'

'That's therapy-speak,' said Agatha defensively.

'None the less, it's true. You'll go to Norfolk but he'll still be there with you until you make an effort to eject him. I hope you don't get involved in any more murders, Agatha, but there are times when I wish someone would murder James.'

'That's a terrible thing to say!'

'Can't help it. Never mind. Anyway, why Norfolk, why this village, what's it called again, Fryfarm?'

'I stuck a pin in a map. You see, this fortune-teller told me I should go.'

'No wonder the churches are empty,' said Mrs Bloxby, half to herself. 'I find that people who go to clairvoyants and fortune-tellers lack spirituality.'

Agatha felt uncomfortable. 'I'm only going for a giggle.'

'An expensive giggle – to rent a cottage. Winter in Norfolk. It will be very cold.'

'It will be very cold here.'

'True, but Norfolk is so . . . flat.'

'Sounds like a line from Noel Coward.'

'I'll miss you,' said Mrs Bloxby. 'I suppose you will want me to phone you if James comes back?'

'No . . . well, yes.'

'I thought so. Let's have some tea.'

Agatha found the day of her departure arriving too soon. All her desire to flee Carsely had left her. But the weather was still sunny and unusually mild, and she had paid a hefty deposit on the cottage in Fryfam, so she reluctantly began to pack suitcases into the boot of her car, and also on the new luggage rack of the roof.

On the morning of her departure, she left her house keys with her cleaner, Doris Simpson, and then returned home to coax Hodge and Boswell into their cat boxes. She drove off down Lilac Lane, cast one longing look at James's cottage, turned the corner and then sped up the leafy hill out of Carsely, the cats in their boxes on the back seat and a road map spread beside her on the passenger seat.

The sun shone all the way until she reached the boundaries of the county of Norfolk and then the sky clouded over the brooding flat countryside.

Norfolk became part of East Anglia after the invasion of the Anglo-Saxons in the fifth century, Norfolk meaning 'Home of the North Folk'. The area was originally the largest swamp-land in England. The higher places were sites of Roman stations. The Romans attempted drainage and built a few roads across the Fens, as the marshland is called. But after the arrival of the Anglo-Saxons, their work was left to decay, and the first effective drainage system was not developed until the seventeenth century, consisting of a series of dikes and channels.

Agatha, used to the twisting roads and hills of the Cotswolds, found all this flatness, stretching as far as the eye could see, infinitely depressing.

She pulled into a lay-by and studied the map. The cats scrabbled restlessly behind her. 'Soon be there,' she called to them. She could not find Fryfam. She took out an Ordnance Survey map of the area and at last found it. She consulted the road map again now that she knew where it was and the name seemed to leap up at her. Why hadn't she seen it a minute ago? It nestled in the middle of a network of country roads. She carefully wrote down the road numbers of all the roads leading to the village and then set off again. The sky was getting darker and a thin drizzle was beginning to mist the windscreen.

At last, with a sigh of relief, she saw a signpost with the legend 'Fryfam' on it and followed its white pointing finger. There were now pine woods on either side and the countryside was becoming hilly. Round another bend, and there was a board with 'Fryfam' on it, heralding that she had arrived. She stopped again and took out the estate agent's instructions. Lavender Cottage, her new temporary home, lay in Pucks Lane on the far side of the village green.

A very large village green, thought Agatha, circling round it. There was a huddle of houses with flint walls, a pub, a church, and then, running along by the graveyard, should be Pucks Lane. The road was very narrow and she drove slowly along, hoping she did not meet a car coming the other way. Agatha was hopeless at reversing. She switched on her headlights. Then she saw a faded sign, 'Pucks Lane', and turned left and bumped along a side lane. The cottage lay at the end of it. It was a two-storey, brick-and-flint building which seemed very old. It sagged slightly towards a large garden, a very large garden. Agatha got stiffly out and peered over the hedge at it.

The estate agent had said the key would be under the doormat. She bent down and located it. It was a large key, like the key to an old church door. It was stiff in the lock, but with a wrench, she managed to unlock the door. She found a switch on the inside of the door, put on the light and looked around. There was a little entrance hall. On the left was a dining-room and on the right, a sitting-room. There were low black beams on the ceiling. A door at the back of the hall led into a modern kitchen.

Agatha opened cupboard doors. There were plenty of dishes and pots and pans. She went back to the car and carried in a large box of groceries. She took out two tins of cat food and opened them, put the contents into two bowls, filled two other bowls with water and then returned to the car to get her cats. When she saw them quietly feeding, she began to carry all her other luggage in. She left it all in the hall. The first things she wanted were a cup of coffee and a cigarette. Agatha had given up smoking in the car ever since she had dropped a lighted cigarette down the front of her blouse one day and had nearly had an accident.

It was when she was sitting at the kitchen table with a mug of coffee in one hand and a cigarette in the other that she realized two things. The kitchen did not have a microwave. Recently Agatha had abandoned her forays into 'real' cooking and had returned to the use of the microwave. Also, the cottage was very cold. She got up and began to search for a thermostat to jack up the central heating. It was only after a futile search that she realized there were no radiators. She went into the sitting-room. There was a fireplace big enough to roast an ox in. Beside the fireplace there was a basket of logs. There was also a packet of fire-lighters and a pile of old newspapers. She lit the fire. At least the logs were dry and were soon crackling away merrily. Agatha searched through the house again. There were fireplaces in every room except the kitchen. In the kitchen, in a cupboard, she found a Calor gas heater.

This is ridiculous, thought Agatha. I'll need to spend a fortune on heating this place. She went out the front door. The garden still seemed very big. It would need the services of a gardener. The lawn was thick with fallen leaves. It was late on Saturday. The estate agents would not be open until Monday.

After she had unpacked her groceries and put all her frozen meals away, she opened the back door. The back garden had a washing green and little else. As she looked, she blinked a little. Odd little coloured lights were dancing around at the bottom of the garden. Fireflies? Not in cold Norfolk. She walked down the garden towards the dancing lights, which abruptly disappeared on her approach.

Her stomach rumbled, reminding her it was some time since she had eaten. She decided to lock up and walk down to the pub and see if she could get a meal. She was half-way down the lane when she realized with a groan that she had not unpacked the cats' litter boxes. She returned to the cottage and attended to that chore and then set out again.

The pub was called the Green Dragon. A badly executed painting of a green dragon hung outside the door of the pub. She went in. There were only a few customers, all men, all very small men. They watched her progress to the bar in silence.

It was a silent pub, no music, no fruit machines, no television. There was no one behind the bar. Agatha's stomach gave another rumble. 'Any service here?' she shouted. She turned and looked at the other customers, who promptly all looked at the stone-flagged floor.

She turned impatiently back to the bar. What sort of hell-hole have I arrived in? she thought bitterly. There was the rapid clacking of approaching high heels and then a vision appeared on the other side of the bar. She was a Junoesque blonde like a figurehead on a ship. She had thick blond – real blond – hair, which flowed back from her smooth peaches-and-cream face in soft waves. Her eyes were very wide and very blue.

'How can I help you, missus?' she asked in a soft voice.

'I'm hungry,' said Agatha. 'Got anything to eat?'

'I'm so sorry. We don't do meals.'

'Oh, for heaven's sake,' howled a much exasperated Agatha. 'Is there anywhere in this village that time forgot where I can get food?'

'Reckon as how you're lucky. I got a helping of our own steak pie left. Like some?'

She gave Agatha a dazzling smile. 'Yes, I would,' said Agatha, mollified.

She held up a flap on the bar. 'Come through. You'll be that Mrs Raisin what's taken Lavender Cottage.'

Agatha followed her into the back premises and into a large dingy kitchen with a scrubbed table in the centre.

'Please be seated, Mrs Raisin.'

'And you are?'

'I'm Mrs Wilden. Can I offer you a glass of beer?'

'I wouldn't mind some wine if that isn't asking too much.'

'No, not at all.'

She disappeared and shortly after returned with a decanter of wine and a glass. Then she put a knife, fork and napkin in front of Agatha. She opened the oven door of an Aga cooker and took out a plate with a wedge of steak pie. She put it on a large plate and then opened another door in the cooker and took out a tray of roast potatoes. Another door and out came a dish of carrots, broccoli and peas. She put a huge plateful in front of Agatha, added a steaming jug of gravy, which she seemed to have conjured out of nowhere, and a basket of crusty rolls and a large pat of yellow butter. Not only was the food delicious but the wine was the best Agatha had ever tasted. She could not normally tell one wine from another, but she somehow knew this one was very special, and wished that her baronet friend, Sir Charles Fraith, could taste it and tell her what it was. She turned to ask Mrs Wilden, but the beauty had disappeared back to the bar.

Agatha ate until she could eat no more. Feeling very mellow and slightly tipsy, she made her way back to the bar.

'All right, then?' asked Mrs Wilden.

'It was all delicious,' said Agatha. She took out her wallet. 'How much do I owe you?'

A startled look of surprise came into those beautiful blue eyes.

'I told you, we don't do meals.'

'But . . .'

'So you were welcome to my food and drink,' said Mrs Wilden. 'Best go home and get some sleep. You must be tired.'

'Thank you very much,' said Agatha, putting her wallet away. 'You and your husband must join me one evening for dinner.'

'That do be kind of you, but he's dead and I'm always here.'

'I'm sorry your husband's dead,' said Agatha awkwardly as Mrs Wilden held up the flap on the bar for her to pass through. 'When you said "our" steak pie, I thought . . .'

'I meant me and mother.'

'Ah, well, you've been very kind. Perhaps I could buy a round of drinks for everyone here?' The customers had been talking quietly, but at Agatha's words there was a sudden silence.

'Not tonight. Don't do to spoil them, do it, Jimmy?'

Jimmy, a gnarled old man, muttered something and looked sadly at his empty tankard.

Agatha walked to the door. 'Thanks again,' she said. 'Oh, by the way, there's these funny dancing lights at the bottom of the back garden. Is it some sort of insect like a firefly you've got in these parts?'

For a moment the silence in the pub was absolute. Everybody seemed frozen, like statues. Then Mrs Wilden picked up a glass and began to polish it. 'We got nothing like that round here. Reckon your poor eyes were tired after the journey.'

Agatha shrugged. 'Could be.' She went out into the night.

She remembered she had left the fire blazing and had not put a fire-guard in front of it. She ran the whole way back, terrified her beloved cats had been burnt to a crisp. She fumbled in her handbag for that ridiculous key. Need to oil the lock, she thought. She got the door open and hurtled into the sitting-room. The fire glowed red. Her cats lay stretched out in front of it. With a sigh of relief she bent down and patted their warm bodies. Then she went up to bed. There were two bedrooms, one with a double bed and one with a single. She chose the one with the double bed. It was covered in a huge, thick duvet. She explored the bathroom. It had an immersion heater. It would take ages to heat water for a bath. She switched it on, washed her face and cleaned her teeth and went to bed and fell into a sound and dreamless sleep.

The morning was bright and sunny. Agatha had a hot bath, dressed and had her usual breakfast of two cups of black coffee and three cigarettes. She let the cats out into the back garden and then, returning to the kitchen, picked up the estate agent's inventory of the contents. Agatha, an old hand at renting property, knew the importance of checking inventories. She wanted all her deposit back, and did not want it defrayed by mythical losses.

Agatha was half-way through it when there was a knock at the door. She opened it and found herself confronted by four women.

The leader of them was a rangy middle-aged woman in a sleeveless padded jacket over a checked shirt. She was wearing corduroy trousers which bagged at the knee. 'I'm

Harriet Freemantle,' she said. 'I've brought you a cake. We all belong to the Fryfam Women's Group. Let me introduce you. This is Amy Worth.' A small, faded woman in a droopy dress smiled shyly and handed Agatha a jar of chutney. 'And Polly Dart.' Large tweedy county woman with beetling eyebrows and an incipient moustache. 'Brought you some of my scones,' she boomed. 'I'm Carrie Smiley.' The last to come forward was youngish, about thirty-something, with dark hair, dark eyes, good figure in T-shirt and jeans. 'I've brought along some of my elder-berry wine.'

'Come in, please,' said Agatha. She led the way into the kitchen.

'They've done old Cutler's place quite nicely,' said Harriet, as she and the others put their presents on the kitchen table.

'Cutler?' said Agatha, plugging in the kettle.

'An old man who lived here for ages. His daughter rents it,' said Amy. 'The cottage was a terrible mess when he died. He never threw anything away.'

'I'm surprised the daughter didn't just sell it. Must be difficult to rent.'

'Don't know about that,' said Harriet. 'You're the first.'

'Coffee, everyone?' asked Agatha. There was a chorus of assent. 'And perhaps we'll have some of Mrs Freemantle's cake.'

'Harriet. It's all first names.'

'As you probably already know, I'm Agatha Raisin. I belong to a ladies' society in my home village of Carsely.'

'A *ladies'* society?' exclaimed Carrie. 'Is that what you call it?'

'We're a bit old-fashioned,' said Agatha. 'And we call each other by our second names.' Harriet was efficiently cutting a delicious chocolate cake into slices and arranging the slices on plates. I'll put on pounds if I'm not careful, thought Agatha. First that ginormous meal at the pub and now chocolate cake.

When the coffee was poured, they all took their cups and plates through to the sitting-room. 'Should I light the fire?' asked Agatha.

'No, we're all warm enough,' said Harriet without consulting the others.

'I think they might at least have had some sort of central heating,' complained Agatha. 'The rental was expensive enough without having to pay for wood.'

'Oh, but you've plenty of wood,' said Polly. 'There's a shed at the bottom of the garden full of logs.'

'I didn't see it. But it was dark when I arrived. Oh, by the way, I saw these odd lights dancing about at the bottom of the garden.'

There was a silence and then Carrie asked, 'Is anything missing?'

'I'm just in the middle of checking the inventory, so I don't know. Why?'

There was another silence.

Then Harriet said, 'We wondered whether you would like to be an honorary member of our women's group while you're here. We're quilting.'

'What's that?' mumbled Agatha, her mouth full of cake. Why wouldn't they talk about those lights?

'We're making patchwork quilts. You know, we sew squares of coloured cloth on to old blankets.'

Competitive as ever, Agatha Raisin would not admit she could not sew. 'Sounds like fun,' she lied. 'Might drop in sometime. It is so very kind of you all to bring me these presents.'

'Tonight,' said Harriet. 'We meet tonight. I'll come and pick you up at seven o'clock, right after evening service. Are you C of E?'

'Yes,' said Agatha, who wasn't really anything but felt that her friendship with Mrs Bloxby qualified her for membership in the Church of England.

'Oh, in that case, I'll see you in church this evening and we'll go on from there,' said Harriet.

Agatha was just about to lie and say she was feeling too poorly to go anywhere, when Polly said abruptly, 'Well, go on. Tell us about your broken heart.'

Agatha reddened. 'What are you talking about?'

'When we heard you were coming,' said Harriet, 'and that you lived in a village in the

Cotswolds, we wondered why you would want to rent in another village and so we decided you had man trouble and wanted to get away.'

I'm going off you lot rapidly, thought Agatha. She smiled round at them all, that sharklike smile which meant Agatha Raisin was about to tell a whopping lie.

'Actually I'm writing a book at the moment,' she said. 'I wanted somewhere to write and have peace and quiet. You see, old friends from London keep dropping down on visits and I don't have enough time for myself. I'll go along with you tonight, but I am afraid I'm going to be a bit of a recluse.'

'What are you writing?' asked Amy.

'A detective story.'

'What's it called?'

'*Death at the Manor*,' said Agatha, improvising wildly.

'And who's your detective?'

'A baronet.'

'You mean you're doing another sort of Lord Peter Wimsey?'

'Do you mind if I don't talk about my work any more?' said Agatha. 'I don't like discussing it.'

'Just tell us,' said Amy, leaning forward. 'Have you had any published?'

'No, this is my first attempt. I am a real-life detective, so I thought I may as well fictionalize some of my adventures.'

'You mean you work for the police?' asked Harriet.

'I occasionally work *with* the police,' said Agatha grandly. She proceeded to brag about her cases. To her irritation, just as she had got to the exciting bit of one of them, Harriet rose and said abruptly, 'Sorry, we've got to go.'

Agatha saw them out. She walked with them down to the garden gate and waved them goodbye. She stayed leaning on the gate, enjoying the sunshine.

Harriet's voice travelled back to her ears. 'Of course she was lying.'

'Do you think so?' Amy's voice.

'Oh, yes. Not a word of truth in any of it. Woman probably can't write a word.'

Agatha clenched her fists. Jealous cow. She would show her. She *would* write a book. Writing was writing and she had written enough press releases in her days as a public relations officer. She had brought her computer and printer with her. She began to feel quite excited. When her name topped the best-seller list, then James would sit up and take notice.

On her way back to the house, she peered over the hedge at the driveway at the side of the house where her car was parked. What had they meant by asking if anything was missing?

She opened the kitchen door and went down to the bottom of the garden, finding a shed behind a stand of trees. It was full of logs. She returned to the kitchen with the cats scampering at her heels. At least they're happy with the place, she thought. She fed them and returned to checking the inventory, but all the while wondering about her visitors. Did they have husbands? They couldn't all be widows.

After she had finished ticking off everything on the inventory, she scraped out the contents of Genuine Bengali Curry into a pot. She would need to buy a microwave. She ate the hot mess and then decided to get down to writing that book.

She set up the computer on the kitchen table, typed in 'Chapter One', and then stared at the screen. She found that instead of writing that book, she was beginning to write down excuses to get out of quilting. 'I suffer from migraine.' No good. They'd all call around with pills. 'Something urgent has come up.' What? And how on earth could she get in touch with them? Mrs Wilden at the pub would know.

She decided to walk down to the pub.

Agatha, as she trudged down Pucks Lane, decided she had better start observing everything about the countryside. Writers did that. The red berries of hips and haws could be seen in the hedgerow to her right. Okay. 'The red berries of hips and haws shone like jewelled lamps . . .' No, scrub that. 'The scarlet berries of hips and haws hung like lamps over the . . .'

Nope, try again. 'Hawthorn berries starred the hedgerow.' No, berries can't star. Flowers can. Who the hell wants to be a writer anyway?

The pub was closed. Agatha stood irresolute. In the middle of the village green was a duck pond, minus ducks. There was a bench overlooking it. She crossed over and sat down and stared at the water.

'Afternoon.'

Agatha jumped nervously. A gnarled old man had sat quietly down beside her.

'Afternoon,' said Agatha.

He shuffled along the bench until he was sitting close to her. He smelt of ham soup and cigarette smoke. He was obviously in his Sunday best, to judge from the old hairy suit, the white shirt and striped tie. His large boots were highly polished.

Then Agatha felt something on her knee, and looking down, saw that he had placed one old hand on it.

Agatha lifted up his hand and placed it on his own knee. 'Behave yourself,' she said sharply.

'Don't you go worriting about that fellow back home who done you wrong. Us'll look after you.'

Agatha rose and strode off, her face flaming. Had the whole village decided she had a broken heart? Damn them all. She would see the estate agent first thing on Monday morning and say she wanted to cancel.

She found a street leading off the far end of the village green which had a small selection of shops. There was a post office-cum-general store like the one in Carsely, an electrical-goods shop, one selling Laura Ashley-type clothes, an antique shop, and at the end, Bryman's, the estate agent. She studied the cards in the window. House prices were less than in the Cotswolds, but not much less.

She wandered back to the village green, as lonely as a cloud, and decided to go back home and spend a useful day unpacking the rest of her stuff.

The gardener called during the afternoon and asked her if there was anything in particular she would like to have done. Agatha said she would like him to sweep the leaves, mow the lawn and keep the flower-beds tidy. He was a young man, muscled and tattooed, with a thick thatch of nut-brown hair. He said his name was Barry Jones and he would call round on the next day. Agatha thanked him and as he turned to go, she said, 'Do you know anything about odd lights? I saw odd little lights dancing around at the bottom of the garden last night.'

He did not even turn around. 'Reckon I don't know nothing about that,' he said and walked away with a rapid pace.

There's something odd about those lights, thought Agatha. Maybe it's some wretched poisonous insect and the locals don't want to put off visitors to the village by telling them about it.

She went back to her housekeeping duties, wondering as she hung away clothes whether the log fires would be enough to keep the house warm in a cold spell. The estate agent should have warned her.

When she realized it was nearly six o'clock, she began to wonder whether she should get out of going to church and then quilting. She checked the TV guide she had brought with her. There was nothing much on. And, she realized, she was lonely.

She locked up and walked round to the church in time for Evensong. To her amazement, in these godless days, the church was full. The vicar's sermon dealt with faith as opposed to superstition, and Agatha's mind drifted back to those lights. There was a closed, inbred, anachronistic feel to this village. All across the world raged fire and floods and famine. Yet here in Fryfam, hatted ladies and suited gents raised their voices in 'Abide With Me' as if nothing existed outside their safe English world governed by the changing seasons and the church calendar: Michaelmas, Candlemas, Harvest Festival, Advent, Christmas.

She waited in the churchyard. Harriet approached her surrounded by the three others she had met earlier. They were wearing the same clothes but had put on hats – Harriet a felt pudding basin, Amy a straw, Polly Dart a tweed fishing hat and Carrie sporting a baseball cap.

Agatha, who had changed into a tailored trouser suit and silk blouse, felt almost overdressed.

'Right,' said Harriet. 'Off we go!'

A couple passed their group, arguing acrimoniously. 'Don't be such a *bore*, Tolly,' said the woman. A waft of Gucci's Envy reached Agatha's nostrils. She paused, looking after the couple. The woman had what Agatha thought of as the 'new' beauty, meaning others admired it. She had blond hair worn down to her shoulders. She was wearing a well-tailored tweed suit, the skirt of which had a slit up one side, revealing a well-shaped leg clothed in a ten-denier stocking – stockings, not tights, for the slit was long enough to show a flash of stocking top. Her eyes were pale blue and well set apart. She had high cheek-bones, but her nose was set too close to her mouth and her long mouth too close to her square chin. He was older, small, plump and choleric, with thinning hair and a high colour.

'Come on, Agatha,' ordered Harriet.

'Who are they? That couple?'

'Oh, that's our squire, self-appointed, made his money out of bathroom showers, and his wife, Lucy. The Trumpington-Jameses. Funny, isn't it,' said Harriet, her voice carrying across the churchyard. 'Not so long ago a double-barrelled name denoted a lady or gentleman. Now it means it's some lower-middle-class parvenu.'

'Aren't you being a bit snobby?' asked Agatha.

'No,' said Harriet. 'They're quite awful, as you'll find out.'

'How will I find out?'

'They'll think it their squire-archical duty to welcome the newcomer. You'll see.'

'Where are we going?'

'My place.'

Harriet's place was on the far side of the green, a square, early Victorian house.

Leading the way into a large, if gloomy, sitting-room, Harriet switched on the lamps and said, 'Anyone for a drink first?' And before a grateful Agatha could ask for a gin and tonic, Harriet said, 'I know, we'll have some of Carrie's elderberry wine.'

Agatha looked about her. The room had long windows and a high ceiling but was crowded with heavy pieces of furniture. The walls were painted a dull green and hung with dingy paintings of horses and dead game.

Amy was getting blankets and boxes of cloth and sewing implements out of a large chest in the corner.

'I think you should share a quilt with Carrie,' said Amy. 'You work on the one end and she'll work on the other. If you sit side by side, you can spread the blanket out between you.'

Harriet returned with a tray of glasses full of elderberry wine. Agatha sipped hers cautiously. It was very sweet and tasted slightly medicinal.

'Are we all widows here?' asked Agatha, looking around. 'No husbands?'

'My husband's in the pub with Amy's and Polly's,' said Harriet. 'Carrie's divorced.'

'I thought the pub was closed on Sundays. I went round at lunch-time and it was closed.'

'Opens Sunday evenings.' Harriet drained her glass and put it back on the tray. 'We'd best get started.'

It should be simple, thought Agatha, as Carrie handed her a little pile of squares of cloth. Just stitch them on.

'Not like that,' said Carrie, as Agatha stabbed a needle into the edge of one. 'You hem it first and then stitch it on and unpick the hem.' Agatha scowled horribly and proceeded to try to hem a slippery little square of silk. Just as soon as it got a stitch in it, the silk frayed at the edges. She surreptitiously dropped it on the floor and picked out a piece of coloured wool. She glanced sideways at Carrie, who was placing neat little, almost invisible, stitches, rapidly in squares of material.

She decided to start up a conversation to try to distract the others from her amateur sewing. 'Mrs Wilden at the pub treated me to an excellent meal last night. She's quite stunningly beautiful.'

'Pity she's got the morals of a tom-cat,' snapped Polly, biting a thread with strong yellow teeth.

'Oh, really?' said Agatha, looking around curiously at the set faces. 'I found her rather sweet.'

'Good thing you're not married.' Amy, sounding almost tearful.

'When did your husband die, Agatha?' asked Carrie.

'A while back,' said Agatha. 'I don't want to talk about it.' She did not want to tell them her husband had been murdered right after he had surfaced from the past to stop her marrying James Lacey. 'I'm still wondering about those lights,' she went on. She noticed with surprise that because of the distraction of talking she had actually managed to hem a square of cloth.

'Have you seen them again?' asked Harriet.

'No.'

'Well, there you are. You were probably tired after the long drive and thought you saw them.'

Agatha gave up on the subject of the lights. She was sure these women probably gossiped easily among themselves. She was the outsider, not yet accepted, and that was putting the brakes on any conversation.

She felt she was being let out of school when Harriet said after an hour, 'Well, that's it for tonight.'

As Agatha was leaving, she stopped to admire an arrangement of autumn leaves in a vase in the hall. Harriet lifted out the bunch of leaves and thrust it at Agatha. 'Take it,' she said. 'I dip the leaves in glycerine so they should last you the winter.'

Agatha walked homewards bearing the leaves. She remembered there was a large stone vase on the floor by the fireplace in the sitting-room. She let herself into the cottage, glad that she had brought her cats for company as Hodge and Boswell undulated about her ankles.

She walked through to the kitchen and put the bunch of leaves on the kitchen counter. She looked out of the window and the dancing lights were there again.

Agatha unlocked the door and walked down the garden. The lights had disappeared.

Muttering to herself, she walked back to the house. Something funny was going on. She had not imagined those lights and there was nothing wrong with her eyesight.

She walked through to the sitting-room to get that vase. It was no longer there. Agatha began to wonder if she had imagined it. She took the inventory out of the kitchen drawer. Yes, there it was under 'Contents of Sitting-Room' – one stone vase.

Agatha suddenly felt threatened. She checked the doors were locked and went up to bed. Her stomach rumbled, reminding her she had not had any dinner, but the thought of going downstairs again frightened her. She bathed and undressed and crawled under the duvet and pulled it over her head to shut out the terrors of the night.

To order your copies of other books in the Agatha Raisin series simply contact The Book Service (TBS) by phone, email or by post. Alternatively visit our website at www.constablerobinson.com.

No. of copies	Title	RRP	Total
	Agatha Raisin and the Quiche of Death	£5.99	
	Agatha Raisin and the Vicious Vet	£5.99	
	Agatha Raisin and the Potted Gardener	£5.99	
	Agatha Raisin and the Walkers of Dembley	£6.99	
	Agatha Raisin and the Murderous Marriage	£6.99	
	Agatha Raisin and the Terrible Tourist	£6.99	
	Agatha Raisin and the Wellspring of Death	£6.99	
	Agatha Raisin and the Wizard of Evesham	£6.99	
	Agatha Raisin and the Witch of Wyckhadden	£6.99	
	Agatha Raisin and the Fairies of Fryfam	£5.99	
	Agatha Raisin and the Love from Hell	£5.99	
	Agatha Raisin and the Day the Floods Came	£5.99	
	Agatha Raisin and the Curious Curate	£5.99	
	Agatha Raisin and the Haunted House	£5.99	
	Agatha Raisin and the Deadly Dance	£5.99	
	Agatha Raisin and the Perfect Paragon	£6.99	
	Agatha Raisin and Love, Lies and Liquor	£5.99	
	Agatha Raisin and Kissing Christmas Goodbye	£6.99	
	Agatha Raisin and a Spoonful of Poison	£6.99	

And available in 2009 . . .

No. of copies	Title	Release Date	RRP	Total
	Agatha Raisin: There Goes the Bride	Oct 2009	£18.99	
	Grand Total			£